One of These Days

One of These Days

Stories

Trent D. Hudley

velizbooks.com

For further information write Veliz Books:
P.O. Box 920243, El Paso, TX 79912
velizbooks.com

ISBN 978-0-9969134-6-1

Cover Image "Recogerse"
by Daniel Barbeito
All rights reserved

Cover design by Silvana Ayala

For Kaidyn,
the soul of my soul

TABLE OF CONTENTS

Armadillos Surrounded the Courtyard

Water seeped through the dry, red earth of the mesa. It crept through the tiny capillaries made by mites and velvet wasps, through the veins made by fire ants, and the tunnels bored by tarantulas and black widows. It bubbled up from kangaroo rat dens and turned the surface of the mesa into an ochre mud pit. The carcasses of the armadillos had begun to surround the biologist's courtyard after the third day of rain.

The biologist peeked out of a window and watched the bodies floating in the water at the rim of the mesa. They bumped into one another and bobbed up and down like cartoon tugboats in an overcrowded dock. Seven-banded armadillos do not ball up like three-banded armadillos, so their short, stiff, pudgy, bone-plated legs stuck straight up from their bloated bellies. The biologist watched through a pair of binoculars to see if any of the legs were moving.

The churning waters below the mesa rushed by carrying all manner of dead things. During the second day of rain the biologist had seen the body of a peccary, and an hour later that of a six-foot sidewinder wash through the gully below him. The branches of sagebrush, yucca, cacti, and mesquites were dragged along, poking above the water like emaciated arms stretching out for help. On the third day he watched a chuckwalla lizard, with Buddha-like acceptance, float by on the barrel of a saguaro.

The biologist did not step outside of his cabin on the mesa when the armadillos started showing up. The first two days of the rain he had tried to maintain a moat around the cabin, but when the first few armadillos washed up against the mesa it frightened him. He didn't know why the appearance of the creatures had affected him so adversely. Being a scientist he felt he should have been teeming with curiosity. But it was how they appeared that he could not categorize in his mind. They had just appeared. They weren't there at one moment and then the next moment they were. He had seen the other things, the snake, the plants, and the peccary coming from a distance. He had seen their point of origin from a distinct and particular position in quantifiable space; he witnessed their linear progression toward the mesa. These things had experiential history in his consciousness. He did not see where the armadillos kept coming from; they were unaccountable. There were not supposed to be armadillos in the area; there had never been any armadillos in the area. It was too barren. Just maroon earth for hundreds of miles in every direction dotted with an occasional mesa or butte. This was Pepsis wasp country. The burrowing habits of Pepsis wasp were what he had been assigned to study, not things that were not supposed to be there. He could not call the institution to find out where the animals had originated because the water had shorted out the wiring connecting the antenna to his radio. He was left with no bearing from which to judge the phenomenon.

Why armadillos? he thought. It would make more sense if it were Gila monsters, blind moles, or even pumas. But armadillos? Armadillos don't belong here.

As the rain continued and the number of armadillos increased, he felt as if he were in a dream, as if the paradigm of physical law was shifting or reversing itself. Armadillos made no sense. The fact that he could not imagine where the creatures were coming from infuriated him as well as frightened him. He had taken this post to catalogue the activities of a known and existing life form. He was there to observe and record, to order and organize. He did not possess the tools to investigate events he was not expecting. Plus, there was just something strange about the beasts. They were not like any armadillo he had ever seen. There was something almost amphibian about them, something old that made his skin feel cold and sweaty. And although they repulsed him, the way they floated, so stiff and rigid, he could not take his eyes off of them. He watched them all day to make sure that they did not move, to make sure they stayed dead. At night it was worse. He tried to sleep, but he kept imagining that he heard the sound of over-sized claws scraping against the outside walls. Then he would get up and sit at the window with his night vision goggles and tranquilizer gun, and watch the puffy, toadstool-white, bodies float around the rim of the mesa like suffocated fish.

On the fifth day of rain, the biologist looked out of the window and saw the hind leg of one of the animals move. Terror struck him and he became transfixed. He did not move from the window day or night. He did not even eat. He stared through the binoculars all day and through night vision goggles all night.

After several days of sitting at the window, the growth of his beard stuck out from his face like tiny quills. Dark purple circles cradled his eyes. The skin of his face stretched across the cheekbones, and the nut-brown tone of his skin faded to beige. Throughout the long hours he labored to discern if the movement of the leg had been an illusion or if it had really moved. Perhaps, he thought, it had only been the flickering reflection of the emerging sun upon the water, or maybe the water itself splashed up against the swollen appendage, or possibly it had just been a stick floating by at that moment. The fear that the things may have just been in some sort of hibernation or suspended animation and could wake up and wander around chilled him. If they were alive, he thought, it would mean that the world was some other thing than he had thought it was, some other place than the place he wanted to be in; and that everything that is, is not really what it is. A pressure like ice forming in his temples grew painfully and spread over the top of his skull and down his neck. He felt dizzy. He stood to get some water from the refrigerator but collapsed.

He woke up startled and confused. It was dark. He jumped up in a panic and rushed to the window; he fumbled for the goggles. The fluorescent green images of the animals still floated and bobbed up and down against the rim of the courtyard. He stared and scrutinized every inch of the creatures for a long while. When he was sure that they were dead, he put down the goggles and lit his lantern. Hunger clawed in his belly. Scrambled eggs sounded like ambrosia. Pulling the eggs from the refrigerator, he dropped one on the floor. He picked up a towel to clean the mess up, but when he turned back around he saw that the egg had already been devoured by a bloated, white, jelly-fleshed armadillo that waddled slowly back into the pantry.

Nothing that Is Not the Moon

At night when I used to walk home alone from work, I was careful to greet everything I saw with the utmost sincerity. It was not because I feared that I would be assaulted or robbed, but because I know that not everything out there is solid. Not everything is fully formed. I see these things; a gracious acknowledgement is the least I can do for my fellow beings, complete and incomplete. I must acknowledge their striving for completeness. They are not ghosts. They are not the end of an existence; they are parts of existences, frozen fragments, and the beginnings of existences. These beings aren't dead; they are struggling for completion. Some of them are true spirits, essences, or rather unformed potentialities that are inexperienced with mass and weight, and if you pay attention and look hard enough you can see their insubstantiality. They are not dilettantes trying desperately to transform themselves by any means. No, they are new, brand new eruptions into being. Quantum anomalies playing copycat with pre-existing forms. People call them ghosts, aliens, angels, devils, and a host of other names, but they are not; they are children of sorts, learning to be in the world. I'm sure there are animals and inanimate objects that fit into this category of existence too. These beings are rare and most usually don't substantiate very long. The ones that manage to complete themselves, the human-formed ones, and remain stable beings usually don't stay in crowded places. They go to high faraway places like the Andes and Himalayas. And because they cannot remember their creation they invent stories, sciences, religions, mythologies to explain their existence. Some of these ideas may or may not become part of the prevailing paradigm of a culture. Still, there are others that are the after-images of traumatic situations, residual beings misplaced, cast off from the normal flow of time. Perhaps one night while walking home from a coffee shop with a chai tea, you have seen a very vivid image of a person or people in the window of an office building from the corner of your eye. When you turn back around you don't see it, so you dismiss it as your imagination. It is an after-image. It is the leftover impression of something that has happened previously. Perhaps a fellow earlier in the day had received a call from his sister that their father committed suicide, or a lady received a call from a hospital that her ten-year-old son has awakened from his five-month coma. It is the after-image you see: a manifestation of an emotional event etched in existence, left out of time. Nothing disappears completely. Some beings slip out of a person when they fall asleep and wander. This is common; that's why we all dream. But, the majority of the beings that walk the streets at night after the bars and clubs have closed, those quiet solitary beings that we avoid or fear, are shades of people who are wholly constituted materially, aspects of flesh and blood beings. But some of these souls, or whatever concept or philosophy you choose to define them through, manifest themselves physically in the waking world. I have touched one, and the memory is visceral. They are lost parts of people trying to find their way back to the host person, or searching for some holistic answer that grants them salvation. These types, these noumenal wanderers, are the majority of these atypical beings. These types are what we're concerned with. When someone tells you they have lost their soul, believe them. Have compassion for these beings. It is imperative that the depth of the last statement be clearly understood, for it is in understanding this concept that the continued existence of humanity rests.

The tragedy of incompleteness, the terror of existential dissolution, and I am not talking in metaphors, I mean the real disintegration of elements of human existence is a quantifiable, qualitative, phenomenon. A real event happening now.

I am not alone with these experiences. I am not alone with this knowledge.

There are others like myself. Others with the ability to encounter the psychosambulist, Soulless Walkers. Although soulless is probably an imprecise term, more poetic than accurate, it will have to suffice for now. We call ourselves Noumenologists. We are of all ages, the youngest among us being only six years old. We are from all races, all genders, and all classes. We have existed since the time of the first civilizations. We have been venerated and we have been persecuted. There is, as of now, only about 100 of us that are known. We only discover one another by chance. I speculate that our ability works like a type of law, possibly connected to the earth's electromagnetic field working on a sub frequency that jacks straight into our neuro-brain system. But, again this is speculation, we have done no type of investigation in this area. I think this because we are drawn to them, the psychosambulist, and them to us. And being as they are so many and we are so few, we, noumenologist, are bound to meet one another eventually. It is how I met Madelyn.

I encountered a young man one night, or rather an aspect of a young man. An aspect should not be looked upon as an inferior part of a whole. Every aspect is as important as every other aspect in that they create the whole and this whole is ever-changing. Regardless, this aspect was particularly damaged. Now it must be known that these aspects manifest themselves as human beings in appearance. They often look like the person from which they have separated and often they do not. I have heard that sometimes they appear as animals or other objects within nature, a sort of reverse anthropomorphization, but I have never encountered one. This being was a thin, bony image. He was probably about 19, 20, 21, I can't be certain. He was of an indeterminate multi-racial origin. His face was drawn and pale. His eyes recessed in deep, black hollows beneath his brows. His clothing, though once nice and from an expensive brand, was slightly tattered and too small. The cuff of the shirt only reached to the middle of his forearm and the legs of the pants stopped a good three inches above his ankle. He wore black dress socks and black wingtip shoes. He was bald, but wore a brown fedora pulled low around his head. Again, I do not know if this is what the man really looked like. Sometimes they appear exactly the way they look in waking life, sometimes it is how they wished they looked, sometimes it is how they view themselves, and sometimes it is chance.

It was dawn, quiet and overcast. A warm, steady rain fell, and a thin mist drifted through the branches of the trees and over the grass hiding the world in a gray haze. It is still comforting, soothing... transporting. I am deeply affected by rain. It is as if something old, mysterious and...important has returned to the world when it is cast in wet, smoky hues. I find it immensely calming. So I decided to take a walk. There is a park the river runs through close to where I lived. I liked to go there when it rained and watch the rain fall into the river and listen to the sound it made. The path to the park is covered with a canopy of evergreens and oaks. The leaves and branches diffused the rain into a fine, light, spray that gave the mist a delicate shine as it floated through the treetops. I walked slowly watching this interplay. Then the emotion hit me like a truck. The aspect's presence, who I shall call Brian, screamed out to me. I had to follow. It's what I do.

Brian sat on a park bench outside the dim orange glow of a street lamp. His rounded shoulders folded inward toward his chest, and his neck, bowed vulture-like, seemed barely able to support his head. He did not look up when I approached him. Detached aspects of people do not know they are not the full person, and when I think about it, it is really not all that strange. Even when we are...whole, and that's probably the wrong word, we do not act or think within our totality. There is always just some aspect of ourselves that seems to sway us one way or another. "Oh my, I didn't mean to do that. That's not me," "I don't know why I ate all the peanut butter, I don't even like peanut butter," "I apologize, I didn't mean those things I said, I was drunk." So I understand this misconception. The whole is really nothing more but a collection of fragments. But when a fragment becomes inflated it becomes troublesome. It dominates the whole. Then sometimes it breaks off, becomes autonomous, and wanders in the world.

"Good morning," I said.

Without moving his head, he looked up at me from the corner of his eye.

"Are you a rain person too? I love the rain. It refreshes me. Makes me feel alive, happy, and whole, do you know what I mean? Every time it rains I have to take a walk so I can be in it."

He turned his head and looked up at me.

"Are you, OK?"

"M'fine."

"You don't look fine. You look rather sad, and... well, down-trodden. What can I do for you?"

It is important when I ask that question that I have the correct tone and eye contact. It is a tone that is not forceful but knowing and revealing. The tone has to let them know that I know something is very wrong; it cannot be judgmental. It can't be insinuating or imply that I know they are not a total being, this can be disastrous and dangerous. They may flee or worse, become hostile. And even though they are not flesh and blood, they are manifested as matter and they have enough solidity to cause physical damage. The tone must reveal that I am sincere. And I must be. Sincerity is of upmost importance. Insincerity is a particularly cancerous vice. It kills important human elements in all parties involved. I would say it is less detrimental to tell a bold-faced lie than to be insincere. To be insincere you are admitting that you lack any type of ability to be compassionate, a horrible thing to experience. To the other person you are saying your being is so unimportant that it elicits no need for me to participate with you in any meaningful way. Aspects are sincere in their need. I must be sincere in my attempt to help.

"My father died. I didn't—" he managed to say before he broke down into tears.

Here's another important difference about aspects. They willingly give information about themselves. If this had been the real Brian, or whatever that person's name really is, I am quite certain that he would have acted aversely to my question. More than likely perceiving it as an inappropriate proposition. This, in turn, may have resulted in an act of violence. It is a strange phenomenon. "Real" people seem to have a deeply existential aversion to admitting to others that they have feelings that make them afraid or sad or confused, as if these feelings somehow reveal a weakness that only children and the so-called "least" among our species are supposed to possess. It is a person who welcomes being a pariah who openly shares feelings.

I had an aunt, on my mother's side, who was like this. And although I had not developed my ability yet, I had a special place in my heart for her. The rest of the family avoided her whenever possible. When the phone rang at our house and the caller ID read Charlotte, we would let it ring until she hung up. If she dropped by unexpected, my sisters and I were hushed and swept into a back room to hide in shadows and silence. What was so wrong with the woman? She liked to talk. She liked to talk about the way she felt and get one to talk about how they felt. She would openly weep after discussing her feelings or after one of us, begrudgingly, talked about how we felt if we were sad. She roared with belly laughter if the discussion were joyful and happy, slam her fist and wring her hands if it were a subject that made us angry. And when she tried, sometimes, to discuss the feeling she had that we tried to avoid her, we insincerely tried to placate her by saying that she was wrong and oversensitive. When aunt Charlotte died we all wept. We all told one another how extremely special she was to us, how much we would miss her, how much we loved her. We cried openly in front of each other and comforted each other, and at the time we were sincere about the grief of our loss, but ultimately it has always seemed hypocritical to me because of how we treated her in life. Aunt Charlotte would have enjoyed her funeral I believe.

What was it that bothered us so much about Aunt Charlotte? Perhaps we were afraid of her. Her ability to feel deeply and sincerely was a threat to us. Our apathy and selfishness and gut-wrenching fear was shown in bold contrast to her honesty and courage, and we resented her for that. My family, like most, does not know how to appreciate unmitigated, emotional honesty, and that inability embarrasses them. It penetrates and unnerves us like the incessant electronic buzz of an alarm clock disrupts sleep, and we belittle those people who are capable of such expression: they are annoying, they are sappy, they are sentimental and unrealistic. Perhaps. But perhaps it is we who are fainthearted and unrealistic in our denial.

Aspects are like Aunt Charlotte. They are the parts of us that need expression of that which is hidden, repressed, and ignored. So they break free and search for expression and understanding, and that is what Brian needed that night.

I sat down next to him. He straightened up and looked at me. I looked him in the eye and just held his gaze for a short moment. I smiled. He nodded his head a bit, wiped his face and slid back into the recess of the bench.

"My father died. He died two days ago. He didn't know me when he died. He didn't remember me, I mean. He had that disease, he had that disease that makes people forget everything they ever knew. I forget what it's called. Christ, it's genetic too, I'm sure."

"Alzheimer's disease."

He looked at me and nodded. "Yeah, that's it." He stared out into the fog still nodding. "Alzheimer's," he said, letting each syllable slide slowly across his tongue. "That's a shit thing to happen to someone. It's a shit thing to happen to anyone. Especially my dad. What the fuck could someone do to deserve to have their entire life wiped away? Deleted, a key stroke and 78 years of life just doesn't fucking exist anymore. How does that happen?

"I mean in the end he didn't know who any of his family was. On his death bed he was surrounded by a room full of strangers. Fucking Christ, imagine that. You could see it in his eyes. He was scared. He knew he was dying, man, and there was a roomful of people and there was no one there for him because he didn't know us. He didn't deserve that. Not one bit of that. He was a good man. He was a damn decent human being and he descended into a pit of shit completely alone without one recognizable face to give him some small bit of comfort. That's shit, man. Just plain shit. He didn't deserve that."

He put his face into his hands and wept convulsively. I placed my hand on his shoulder.

"He was a good father. We didn't see eye to eye on stuff. Lifestyle and choices, politics mainly. That influenced everything else I guess. It kept us separated. Kept me separated from most of my family really.

But especially him. Shit, man you know the story. Same old shit. Father and son estranged because of differences of opinion. Opinion. Nothing substantial, nothing real or right, just opinions.

"I went to the family get-togethers on the major holidays. Which always, of course, ended with argument. Then I just started staying away completely. The strife wasn't worth it, you know. My sister called about six months ago and told me he was losing his mind. That's exactly what she said. 'Dad's losing his mind. You need to come see him before it's completely gone. So I'm thinking he's going crazy, you know."

He looks at me with his tongue sticking out of his mouth, his eyes rolling back and forth and his finger pointed at his head making the 'I'm crazy' twirling motion. He leaned back on the bench and turned his face to the sky. He started laughing.

I removed my hand from his shoulder and smiled.

"What the fuck is a person supposed to make of that? 'Dad's losing his mind.'" I'm thinking he's wandering around the house naked, drooling, and chasing mom around with a semi hard pecker, you know. But I went anyway. I thought she was overreacting, but she wasn't. And fuck, he was crazy in a way. Crazy in a way that unless you're losing your mind you'll never understand; you know what I mean? What the fuck did he feel knowing he was disappearing? What the hell does somebody do with a fact like that? In a certain amount of time you are going to completely forget everything and everybody you know and live in fear and confusion on top of the fear and fucking confusion you already live in. You'll even forget to go to the toilet and take a shit and piss; you'll be looked at by people with sad pity and be treated like a child. You will become a burden to your loved ones. Christ I can't even imagine. What the fuck would that do to a person? That's got to drive you crazy in some sense of the word, you know.

"When I first went to see him he'd slip in and out of it. And a few times when we weren't baiting each other and we were quiet and calm, he admitted that he knew he was losing it. He didn't say it, but I could tell he was afraid, he was damn afraid and sad as hell. But I blew it off, 'You'll be alright, dad. Don't worry about it.' That's what I said. Goddamn, that's all I said."

He stood up, bent over and started to retch. I suppose if it had been the total Brian he would have vomited. He stayed bent over with his hands on his knees swaying a bit, sporadically retching and spitting nothing onto the ground. He tottered and fell back onto the bench. His arms fell limp at his sides and he rested his head on the back of the bench. He stared up at the trees, his mouth slightly agape with a sort of half grimace half smile.

"I stayed away for the most part. Just...stayed away. I didn't want to deal with it. Pure and simple. I just didn't want to deal with it. He was a burden."

He bent over again and started to wench.

"He was a burden to my life," he said through coming tears. "I quit going by because I didn't want to deal with him. And Christ, it wasn't even because I didn't want to watch him deteriorate. I just...I just didn't want to be bothered. What does that say, huh? What the fuck does that say? He was my father. I was his son. He was alive and now he is not. I wasted the time I had with him, and I have no idea why now. Whatever reasons I thought so important are gone with him. That's how goddamn all important it was."

He straightened up and leaned his head on the back of the bench again. Rain fell upon his face, and he wept. Then he yelled. It was a sound unlike anything I had ever heard. The physiology of an aspect is not sinew, blood and bone, it is something else. I don't know exactly what but it's something constructed outside of or maybe encompassing the entire gamut of human emotional experience. When Brian yelled it was from the bowels of human existence. I cowered a bit and scooted away from him. Something that strong, that concentrated, that powerful, is frightening. And I was tempted to run away. I understand why people are afraid in the face of overwhelming emotion. It is hard, it is fearful, it is costly. You can't experience pure emotion and not be affected by it. The ego isn't built for that. Even joy can be costly. But I didn't run. My job is to stay, to feel, to help. He bent back over, his arms limp at his side and his face on his knees. I placed my hand on his shoulder and massaged it lightly. It may seem strange, these physical actions, touching his shoulder and so forth. If an aspect has no flesh, how can touching them have any affect upon them? I don't honestly know, but like it would work for a full human, it works for an aspect. I speculate that it performs a similar function as talking calmly does. They are, or I think they are, emotional centers, and touch acts like words in comforting them. Again this is just speculation. Because to be honest, we don't really know what they are exactly.

Regardless. Something strange happened then. It had never happened before. It has happened several times since, but it alarmed me at the time. As I massaged his shoulder, my hand slipped through his body. His body began to waver, then became transparent, and then disappeared. I jumped up startled and looked around. Foolishly, I even looked under the park bench, as if he, like a child, was hiding there.

"Brian?" I whispered.

"It happens," a voice said behind me.

I turned and there was Madelyn.

"He's entered back into consciousness. He woke from sleeping or from his daydream or whatever was occupying his conscious mind," she said.

I didn't know what to say. I just stared at her confused.

"He's integrated back into his whole-self, you know what I mean? You new at this or something?" she asked.

I was confused still. Not about what she was saying but that she obviously could see aspects too. It was exciting, and alarming, and to be honest, a bit annoying that there was someone else who had this ability. I wasn't as unique as I thought I was. It was exciting and alarming for the same reasons. The idea that there were other people with this ability opened up a... a new universe of possibility. It transcends everything we thought we knew about ourselves and the world and space and time and well... what it means to be. The potential was staggering and I actually felt a bit dizzy as these thoughts raced through my mind. In an instant I realized that nothing is necessary, reality is elastic, malleable, created, as well as discovered. There are things we do not know, lots of things, and there are things we have not yet realized, and that is the greatest of opportunities. A real basis for... hope, if you will. Just imagine. I realize to try to solidify a point of view about the world is a type of suicide. How much did I miss clinging to one point of view about reality? Oh so very, very much.

But I realized, with a searing clarity in the same instant, the possibility of abuse of an ability like this. What manipulation and corruption could be accomplished with power like this? What could a group of people with the ability to influence others emotionally do to a society? A nation? The world? The usual suspects flashed through my thoughts: politicians, corporations, serial killers, and those types, and just the petty ego-driven meanness people are subject too. And this flash of fear wasn't unfounded as I found out years later. A young man, with our ability, who had been spurned by a young woman in front of her friends after he'd asked her to prom encountered an aspect of her and convinced her to kill herself. Days later he was overwhelmed with guilt and killed himself. But the tragic matter of fact is that two lives were lost. As usual humanity's paltry, selfish desire twisted a power with miraculous potential to help and create into a force of destruction. I often wonder if we are incapable of doing otherwise. Yet, it is reassuring that nothing of the sort has happened again since... yet.

But beyond the multitude of ideas that bombarded my consciousness at this time, the detail that was most distracting and underlined all my discombobulation was the intensity of Madelyn's beauty. Yet, as arresting and startlingly pleasing as her physical appearance was, especially her smile, it was her manner that evoked promise, and I committed myself to her forthwith.

"I was coming here to meet with him again, but you got here first," she said.

I didn't respond. I continued to stare at her, with, what she claimed later, was an expression as if I had just stepped in dog feces.

"You are new. You didn't know there are others like yourself, huh? Wow. I'm jealous. I wish I was in your shoes right now. I remember that luscious sense of divine confusion. So liberating, but spooky, right?"

I nodded.

"You should sit down before you fall, honey. You look like your mama just told you there was no Santa Claus."

I sat. It helped. I regained a bit of my composure, but I couldn't take my eyes off her. She looked back at me, her right eyebrow cocked as if questioning my intentions. Then she smiled. I managed an odd contortion of my lips that I thought felt like a smile. She laughed and patted my shoulder.

"You'll be alright, man." She said. "Is this your first time out? Was ol', what'd you call him?"

"Brian."

"Brian. Was he your first one?"

"No," I said, shaking my head at the same time.

"How long you known you could do this? How many of them have you encountered?"

"About three years, I suppose. I've engaged with over a hundred I would guess."

"Whoa, really? And you've never encountered another person like yourself, ever?"

I shook my head, staring at her face trying to solidify her in my memory.

"That's wild. Do you only stay in this area? Have you gone outside this neighborhood?"

"I've been to Greece and Viet-Nam, and about six other states on vacation, and I've encountered aspects in all those places, but never anyone like me, or you."

"Hmm. I wonder if that means something. There's more of us. I know five others. I've met one in Peru, one in Kenya, one in Philadelphia, Taos, and Steven's Point, Wisconsin. So I know for sure there are at least seven of us."

"What does it mean?"

"What does what mean?"

"When I told you I have never met others like us. You said you wondered if it means something. Do you think there's something wrong with me? Maybe I'm not... I don't know normal?"
She broke into laughter.

"Well, man. If you think walking around at night talking to detached parts of people's psyches is anything normal..."

"I mean, normal as far as our abilities are concerned, is there something wrong with mine, is there—"

"Slow down, cowboy. I was just thinking out loud. I don't know what's normal. I only know what we can do and why we do it. And you know why too. Listen, I don't like standing out in the rain talking to strangers about paranormal abilities we share. Let's go get some coffee. I'm getting cold."

So I went with her. And I've been with her ever since.

It is hard to put into words what it meant to know there were others that shared my abilities. At first, as I said, I was a bit annoyed. I wasn't special anymore. I couldn't find comfort and meaning in my uniqueness, my sense that I was chosen, alone, to free the world from its pain. The feeling that I was unique afforded me a quality of self-pity I was quite fond of. I liked to imagine my ability alienated me from the rest of humanity, the artist rejected by the masses. But beneath that was a genuine feeling of loneliness. I was incapable of sharing this experience with anyone I knew. Who would believe me? They'd think I was crazy. I couldn't afford that. Being able to share our thoughts and feelings about our experiences is what builds lasting relationships. The commonality of experience is the basis for creating meaningful relationships, which in turn validates our sense of self-worth. And the greater those experiences and their effects upon us, the greater the need to share them. I was not a social recluse. I had friends, I had other experiences I shared with them, we had fun together; I was not bogged down with a deep, terrible sin, but there was always a feeling of not being completely part of their world because of this secret I had. And that's it. I had a secret. I had experiences that I could not talk about, and it crouched in the back of my mind with a dark presence. It was, if not painful, disturbing, and at times stultifying. A secret alienates a person more so than anything else. I will speculate, that 70-80% of all the aspects noumenologists encounter are aspects of loneliness caused by an obstacle blocking the ability to communicate experience. Loneliness stems from secrets. The greater the secret, the deeper the alienation. The victims of traumatic experiences, violence, sexual abuse, war, neglect, imprisonment, oppression of any type that denies or distorts the actualization of expression and affirmation, live in a very different world than most of us. These experiences permeate every aspect of their lives. They exist in a prison, enclosed in a cell of incommunicable being. They are alone with horrible secrets. It is a terrible feeling to have, loneliness.

All loneliness is not caused by traumatic experiences, but that does not mean it cannot be just as debilitating. The first person I encountered, the first time my ability manifested itself, was a very lonely woman, whom I call Sarah. For two weeks I had been struggling with a severe case of insomnia. Nothing I did worked to help me sleep. I took pills, drank liquor, meditated during the day, exercised after work, took warm baths, and a number of other strategies researched and suggested by friends, nothing worked. One night I decided to walk. I had no particular destination, I just started to walk. When I walked outside the air felt charged. I had never felt anything like it so it's hard to explain. They, the air, the ground, the objects around me, had a feeling. I could feel them; I could feel their presence. It was as if thin tendrils of electricity were being emitted from everything around me and I could feel them dancing over every inch of my body. I didn't know it, but I was experiencing the world with an extra non-physical sense, like a snake tasting its world, or a dolphin perceiving through echolocation, or how some eels and other fish detect the world through electrical impulses. This is another reason I now believe that our ability is based on electromagnetism. The feeling was one of calmness and anxiety. It was unnerving to feel this without any known cause. The mind and the body become habituated to experiencing the world in a particular way and any new experience always comes with a bit of apprehension. But it lasted only a minute. The calm was euphoric. I felt energized, aware...opened. My fatigue disappeared and I felt as if I could walk forever. I strutted into the night.

In front of an all-night convenience store, I noticed Sarah standing next to a pay phone with her arms crossed, staring out at the few cars that passed by on the main thoroughfare. In my jovial mood I smiled and said good evening; she looked at me quizzically. I got a bottle of water and tried to chat with the cashier, whose tired eyes never once looked at me. I looked at Sarah through the window and it seemed that I could see the street through her. I stared harder and she seemed to flicker. I rubbed my eyes.

"Two dollars," the cashier said, but I just kept staring at Sarah. A car passed on the street and even though I was looking at Sarah's back I saw the car through her.

"Hey man, the water is two bucks," the cashier said irritated.

I paid the man and left, I stared at Sarah as I walked out the store. I could see the dim outline of the phone through her. I kept staring at her as I walked. I was a bit afraid. A cold chill ran through me when I thought I might be seeing a ghost. But the way she looked back at me was pleading. I stopped. She was a handsome woman, probably in her mid-forties. She had dark circles, almost black, under her eyes and she looked as if she hadn't slept for months. She had thin black hair, but it was dirty and greasy as if she hadn't washed it in weeks. It hung around her face and gave her the appearance that it was melting off her head.

"Are you ok?" I asked.

She shook her head and tried to smile. "I don't think so. I don't think I'm OK at all," she said, her eyes tearing up.

I walked back over to her.

"Are you hurt? Are you lost? Can I help you?" I asked.

She shook her head. She looked at me with those sad, pleading eyes and the thin smile turned into a grim line etched across her face.

"Is there someone you need to call? Do you need change to call someone? I don't think that phone works, but I'm sure the cashier will let you use the phone. Here, I'll go ask him."

I opened the store door and stuck my head in and asked if she could use the phone. The cashier put his hands over his face, rubbed his temples and sighed. He looked at me with repulsion.

"Can who use the phone?"

"This woman," I said and pointed at her.

"Come on, man. For Christ's sake give me a break OK. I've had a long fucking day and I don't need this shit. You can't use the business phone. If you need to use a phone, use the pay phone. Give me a dollar; I'll give you some quarters. You use the phone, go home and take your meds, and everything will be cool. Otherwise, I can call the cops and they can deal with you."

"Listen, sir, this woman just needs to use a phone. She's got no money and—"

"OK, OK, I'm done with this. I'm calling the cops," he said and lifted the phone receiver.

Then it hit me. He couldn't see her. Only I could see her. I didn't know what to do. I didn't know what to think. I was immobilized with incomprehension. I looked back and forth from him to her a few times before I heard him on the phone with the police dispatcher. I stared intently at her. She was translucent. But somehow I knew she wasn't a ghost, she wasn't a hallucination, or a real person. I don't know how I knew this, but I did. And the strange thing was I didn't feel any type of apprehension anymore. I felt the need to know what this... being was.

"Ma'am, maybe I can help you get back home, would that be OK?" I asked and placed my hand on her shoulder to gently guide her away from the store before the police showed up. And that was when it happened.

I don't know any other way to describe the experience except that I absorbed her, or rather she absorbed me. I was her. Her perceptions, her attitudes, her memories were mine (I knew her real name then, of course, but I will continue to call her Sarah). It was both terrifying and exhilarating. I was aware of not being her too, I mean, I suppose, and it still doesn't quite explain the experience, I had a dual consciousness. I was Sarah who realized I wasn't Sarah, but me being Sarah. I was Sarah aware of being watched and understood by another presence, but that presence was me not aware or able to identify with my own memories of who I considered myself to be. That's the best I can do to explain it. And this was like non-being, or rather, being without a self. Just a sort of... pure experience. I am mediating this experience through my conscious mind, from my memories right now. But there was no mediating consciousness during the absorption. If you are confused, that's because I am still confused about it myself. It is not a common experience among people with the ability. I was unprepared and inexperienced. I let the construction of myself, the thing I call my identity, become deconstructed in the confrontation with a more adamant structure, that being Sarah's construction of her identity. That's not to say she had a stronger personality than me. Her idea of her personality was more inflexible than my idea of myself. She clung to the construction of identity that she had created throughout her life, and anything outside of that construction's perceptions was unimaginable to her. My more adaptable identity, and the inexperience with this new facet of my ability, caused my construct of myself to break down and incorporate into hers. That is a result of having this ability, for better or worse. When others first manifest their ability there is some sort of psychic mechanism that dampens the process of a full absorption. They manifest a deep empathy with the particular emotion that the aspect represents, but that is it. Only about 2% of us have the ability to be or to absorb personality constructs. It's not a power to be used frivolously, and we only do it in extreme cases. But I didn't know this at the time I encountered Sarah. The problem with conveying this experience is the problem of language. There is no language, in the sense that we understand it and the way that we use it right now, capable of communicating experience devoid of a mediating conscious. It is, I suppose, like the Buddhist story of the turtle trying to explain to the fish what it is like to walk on land. The fish has no reference to make a comparison, and thus no understanding. So let it suffice for me to say it happened. There is no other evidence that I can offer.

Nine days prior, Sarah had walked in on her husband and another woman. They were in the bed she and her husband slept in. In the bed where I had conceived our child eighteen months before. She heard them when she entered the house. The dirty language the woman was using stopped her at the foot of the stairs leading up to our bedroom. The intensity of her husband's panting and groaning was something she hadn't heard since they first started dating ten years ago. I knew what was going on. What else could it be when you hear a woman squealing "Fuck me harder." in your house and it isn't you? She wasn't going to walk upstairs, but she had to see it. She had to see him doing it to solidify it in her mind, to make it real from the dream she felt she was in. Something so careless and commonplace, something so unoriginally banal, but so deeply hateful and disrespectful couldn't possibly be taking place in her house. It would only mean that everything that I had so desperately tried not to believe was absolutely true about the world and myself. How could the human being that I willingly, enthusiastically, bared all that I thought was honest, authentic and important about myself, just fling it to the wayside like a shit-stained rag. It meant nothing to him. It meant nothing to anyone, not even really myself, if I could be fooled so easily for so long. Her body felt as if it were encased in an iron shell. It took deliberate effort to move her legs from one step to the next. Her vision blurred and her breath came in short, hot rasps. She held onto the banister to steady herself. The distance from the foot of the stairs to the top landing stretched a mile in front of her. She didn't know if she had the strength to make it to the top. But she did, and in that hyper awareness produced by fear she slid silently along the hall wall to her bedroom and peeked in the crack. I hated myself for thinking it, but I was worried that he would be mad at me if I walked in on them. So I peeked through the crack in the door. She was on top of him, the way he liked it. She was bent over him and he was holding her face between his hands and kissing her. The kiss was long and passionate. And that ripped through me with jagged intensity, more than the fact that he was inside of her. There was feeling in it. Deep feeling in that kiss. There was sincere appreciation of each other in the way their lips touched. Even if it was just for that moment, that instant that their mouths pressed against each other's, it was apparent that they adored, in the deepest sense of the word, one another. I got dizzy and my vision turned pale white. I forced myself to remain standing. The fear of being discovered, and the fear of the humiliation of them seeing me peeking at them through the door kept me from falling to the floor.

She left that day. She left her clothes, she left the house, she left her child at the daycare and she left Delaware and travelled as far as she could make it in her 1998 Ford Escort. She got to Denver and stayed at a Comfort Inn. She stayed in her room in the dark, dissolving. And in that room she recreated the mythology of her life. I have never felt anything more paralyzing than the terror at the core of Sarah's being. She conceived herself as a small dim point of white, an absence of anything in a universal expanse of darkness. Imagine a pale fetus. A fetus in the stage of development in which it could be any creature, a human, a fish, a cat, a pig. It pulsates weakly like the last dying beats of a failing heart. It lives strictly because it is alive. It will not develop further. It will not grow; it will not die. It will exist alone in perpetual darkness. It was the existential metaphor she had created for herself. The loneliness was crushing

visceral...

Indescribable.

There was nothing but a dim, formless, vibration of life itself. There was no meaning attached to it. It was the impersonal force of bare life. An abstraction stripped of its function. Mere energy, existing in a chance configuration. She was an unlucky roll of the dice Einstein said God doesn't roll.

And she had held this horror at bay most of her life. A single, unimaginative act of betrayal had flung her into a realm that had, for as long as she could remember, pulsated against the walls of her conscious mind. It had never been as fully actualized as this. She had only felt it as a constant irrational apprehension about her life in general. A type of knowledge that life was not at all the way people tried to live it and represent it. She had always been acutely aware of the fear that emanated off other people like an odor. She dismissed it as her own little neurotic quirkiness because the idea that everyone was as afraid and uncertain as she was, was to admit to herself that all the things that people considered so important: society, the foundation of a civilization, was a desperate sham to stave off, or rather fool ourselves that anything really fucking mattered. And at a precise time within the moments of her life she had decided that it all really didn't mean anything.

I had never before, or since, felt an emptiness so complete. I stumbled and fell spilling the water I held. This all swept through my mind in a brief flash. But, and I guess it is the function of my gift, I also knew that she was free. Everything in her previous life that had so haunted her was rendered powerless. She had sunk into the darkest realm of her existence. There was nothing beyond that but death and she had rendered death meaningless too. She was free to recreate herself, to recreate her perceptions, recreate meaning, to build a whole new paradigm. We walked for a long while and discussed this. I don't know exactly how long we walked, but the sun was just starting to lighten the night sky when I saw a quarter on the ground. I bent to pick it up and when I straightened back up she was gone.

I still wonder what became of Sarah. I never encountered her again as I have many other aspects. I am hoping that I may have helped her in some way. I like to imagine that she remembers me as some odd dream figure that encouraged her to change, and that she is a successful artist or writer or entrepreneur reunited with her child and living full and aware and with deep appreciation for life. But there is also a dark, fearful fantasy that haunts me at times: that she swallowed a handful of sleeping pills and her aspect disappeared because she ended her own life. That the aspect was just wandering the world as she slipped into sleep before she slipped into death. Sarah is a part of me. Her being branded itself into mine that night. She remains there to remind me.

Maddy said something to me once that has stayed with me since, people, she said, don't need love, they need to feel respected. You can love something or someone and have no respect for them whatsoever. You can't love a stranger, but you can respect their being. Love is misunderstood and exclusive. Our estimation of it is overrated. It's naïve to believe that you can love everybody. You can't. Love involves time that we don't have to give to everyone we meet. And unconditional love only applies to parents and their children. There are conditions to love and it is only under those conditions that we do love, when those conditions disappear we can't still love someone, but we can still respect them. Even if love ends in hate, once the hate is gone there can still be respect. Another's existence can always be acknowledged. The power to empathize deeply with another is an innate, dormant power within the human being. It is not some special gift bestowed upon a chosen few. Noumenologists's abilities may just be the beginning of a new form of evolution. Mutations always start in a few before they are adapted by the rest of the species. The rational, reasoned perception of the world is a byproduct of the irrational and the fantastic. Objects, ideas, concepts are created and agreed upon after they are conceived through stretches of the imagination which have nothing to do with reason and rationale. They become reasonable as we try to figure out a place for them within our limited conception of reality. The weird and the strange are the basis for the factual. Reality is weird, even the limited, consensual reality in its structure is weird and irrational. This is a natural potential in all of us that needs to be manifested if we are to survive.

One night Maddy and I were out late. We walked at night in case there were aspects to meet. We would inevitably meet one or two people a night. Meeting one or two aspects is a rather slow night. The average is about six a piece. Now I must say, there is a particular characteristic our ability bestows upon us. The previous statement could be construed that it had been our nightly job to go out and look for the sad and downtrodden. That what we did at night was like a second job. This is not the case at all. It is just what we, Noumenologists, do. Just as one might choose to paint a picture, write a story, play an instrument, we encounter aspects. We enjoy it. Our ability allows us to survive on a minimal amount of sleep and food. It is like a type of human photosynthesis. We gain energy from the aspects we encounter. But recently things have changed. There has been an increase in the number of aspects that are out at night. And they are different. I cannot pinpoint this change. It is like...absence. At times it seems that some element of humanity is missing, that the emotion of the aspect is not an emotion but a sort of distortion or lack of emotion. It is hard to communicate. It is something viral. Not just viral in the sense that something spreads quickly, which is a worrisome idea, but viral in that they are constructed like a virus. There seems to be something dormant but infectious inside them, but they need a host to activate the infection. And like a virus, they mutate. A few times, before this night Maddy and I were walking, when I connected with an aspect, there was nothing there. It was not the terror of nothingness Sarah felt, there was nothing there. This aspect was something new. These beings aren't quantum anomalies, or temporal residue. They are formally unclassified, but that is unimportant right now, what is important is that they changed and the affect they now have on us. It is as if they appropriate something from us as opposed to us giving something to them, as it had been in the past. After dealing with this aspect, I felt uncharacteristically tired, and for a short time, sad, afraid, angry. It is alarming. It is hard to make a distinction between these new aspects and a normal aspect. This new creature, I'm not confident we can define it as a "being," has caused a wave of concern within the noumenological community, and a bit of fear, which is understandable. It is rumored that one of us, a new member, whom I hadn't met, encountered one of these new aspects and lost her ability to the thing. It, for lack of a better analogy, sucked the life out of her. Now, it is rumored, she, the new member, walks among the tortured aspects we normally encounter. I have also heard that a few of our members have resigned their post and no longer use their ability.

That night that Maddy and I were out, we were walking on the path beside the river that runs on the edge of downtown. There is a hill off the path that we like to go to because we can see the lights of the city on one side and listen to the sound of the river coming from the other side. We sat down on the small rocky outcropping we like and leaned into one another. An aspect appeared just below us and started his way up the hill towards us. We smiled at one another. We were eager to engage with him. We let the aspect choose between us when we are together. Another aspect appeared behind us, and then another behind him. They kept appearing until there were about fifteen of them. We were unnerved. We looked at one another. We saw the worry in each other's eyes. We saw the doubt. And the doubt, so alien in our experience, brought with it fear. We were, for the first time, afraid to do what it is we do.

The strange thing about these aspects, and I believe it is what defines them from a normal aspect, is that they did not approach us. They did not seek consideration, they just shambled around us and one another aimlessly. We avoided them on our way back down the hill. We didn't know if they were all the new type of aspect, but we didn't want to take the risk to find out which ones were normal. And this turned the fear to self-doubt. We hurried down the hill. There were more on the path, and even more wandering in the downtown streets.

We were silent when we got home. We locked the door and went to bed. We avoided eye contact with one another, but in the darkness of the bedroom, we clung close under the covers.

We have not gone out at night in months. We talk and try to convince ourselves we need to do more studies before we can be effective again. We make calls and plan meetings over Facebook and emails with other members of the Noumenological community, but the plans and meetings never come to fruition. The truth is we are afraid, and the fear is a secret we will not admit to one another. We do not know what to do. I do not know what to do. Nothing is done.

Pieces

The only light in the room was from the television, a pale, blue-white haze suspended in the surrounding darkness like a patch of metallic mist. Elder DeVille, wrapped in the mist, sat naked, except for his plaid boxer shorts and a can of Pabst beer. Stiff and motionless in his recliner, he stared, unblinking, forward. The television cast gray, flickering shadows across his body, and the sound, turned down low, suffused in his head with the voices from the other room. The images from the television paraded in front of his vision in disconnected flashes of color. A collage of sight and sound swirled around his head like a thin cloud of smoke.

He could hear his sister Mary's voice, thin, soft, and airy, as if it were carried on a breeze from some great distance away. He knew the voice was his sister's, and somewhere in his consciousness he knew she was in the next room, but as he stared into the television screen the words seemed to come from the mouth of a tiny animated chameleon—garbled, only a few words distinguishable, old words, repetitious words, words like "about time he... money... grown man... job." The words shot into his head like bb's, then ricocheted off the perimeter of consciousness and bounced away into the outlaying darkness. Elder stared. David Muir's face seemed to hover ethereally in front of him, and his mouth moved to the voice of Elder's mother. "I've been trying so hard, but he doesn't respond to me. He walks around the house like a zombie all day. I think he might need... well... help... a doctor of some kind, maybe." Elder chuckled, sighed loudly, then closed his eyes. The mingling of the television's sound and the voices slowly began to fade and recede into some far away region of his mind until there was only silence and the dissolving after-image of a reporter in the foreground with the desert landscape of some foreign country behind him.

The beer can hit the floor with a dull, muffled smack. Elder opened his eyes slowly. He looked to his empty hand then to the floor where the can wobbled back and forth in a small puddle of beer. On the television, a tornado was tearing through some small Mid-western town. Elder turned off the television and sat staring, unblinking, forward into the dark.

He tried to get up but the familiar tugging sensation kept him in the chair. It felt like his entire body was having a muscle spasm from the tip of his toes to his stomach; even in his brain he felt the twitching. He knew he would have to wait until the thing separated itself before he could move. It only took a minute or so and he was becoming used to it. He stood up and stared down at the transparent apparition in the recliner. It was him—a thin, pale, shade of himself sitting there exactly like he had been seconds ago, flickering slightly as if it were a bad picture on the television—sitting there in his boxer shorts staring, unblinking, forward. They were all over the place. Holographic, phantom selves, bits of himself spewed throughout the house and city, frozen in whatever activity he had been doing when it decided to dislodge itself. Always quiet, always thin and pale, always staring, unblinking forward as if they were hypnotized by some distant vision. There was one lying on his bed naked, staring, wide-eyed, almost frightened, up at the ceiling, there was one in the shower staring down at the drain, one at his desk—his elbows on the desk and his chin resting in the palm of his hands, staring out the window. There was one at the kitchen table, one on the porch smoking a cigarette, one at the bus stop, one on a bench in front of the duck pond at the park, one on a bar stool at Milton's Lounge, one on at least three different buses, and two at the public library in the K of the fiction section. They seemed to be everywhere lately, and he was the only one who could see them. He asked his mother once if the parts of himself that he left around the house bothered her. She only stared at him with wide, pleading eyes on the verge of tears. He didn't seem to disturb them either. Several times he tried to get them back inside of himself by taking the exact same pose that they were frozen in. He would stand or sit, with his eyes closed and concentrating on trying to draw the image back into himself. It never worked. So he moved around them so as not to disturb them. He slept on the floor in a sleeping bag, used the bathroom in the basement, and sat across from the one at the kitchen table. Now he would have to find a different chair to watch television in. He sighed and walked into the kitchen where his sister and mother sat.

They quit talking when he entered. They looked up at him, silent, and he looked at them. His sister put out her cigarette, exhaled a cloud of smoke and eyed him with one eye closed through the cloud. She scooted her chair back from the table, crossed her legs and arms and looked at him. Elder saw that she wore the same white and beige tartan skirt that she had worn ten years ago to their father's funeral. He noticed that the seam was coming undone at her hip and that she had a run in her stocking. He wanted to embrace her and tell her he loved her, and that he always had and always would. He smiled his crooked smile and his sister sighed. "I'm going out," he said, and walked upstairs to dress.

They resumed their conversation and the voice of his mother and sister drifted around inside his head. As he walked up the stairs the voices dissipated into soft white noise in the back of his mind. He stopped outside the door of his room and stared into it. He saw his alarm clock and was reminded of waking up that one morning, how long ago had it been he couldn't recall, it could have been yesterday or ten years ago; he just remembered feeling that something was missing. It had been a vague, nagging, suspicion that he had forgotten something important. He lay in bed staring at the red LED numerals on the clock face. It was 5:28 am. Something was different. Something definitely had changed. He didn't know what; it wasn't a conscious knowledge, just a feeling, a strong intuition. Gray, phantom images of the incessant monotony of his daily routine played across his mind's eye like an old newsreel in slow motion. The thought of engaging in anything caused a knot in his stomach. He wrapped his arms tight around himself and curled up into a semi-fetal position. The electronic insect buzz of the alarm erupted—the knot in his stomach exploded and diffused into his body, thick, gray and slow like a liquid metal cooling in his veins. He felt unbearable.

The smell of bacon wafted up to his room with the flat monotone of some muzak his mother had playing on the radio. He dreaded having to look his mother in the face. She was the last person in existence that he wanted to see at that moment. He pictured her shuffling around the kitchen, as she had done every morning for what seemed like eons, still in her quilted, powder blue housecoat with the dirty, laced collar unfurling itself around her neck. It was the same scene he had witnessed since he was a kid. Everything the exact same, except the skin around his mother's neck, which had become looser and the spots on her hands, which had become darker. But there would be the same ceramic blue plate, the same wheat toast, two strips of bacon, scrambled eggs and orange juice, and the same happy smile that too honestly revealed the damages of her life. The image caused his neck and shoulders to ache. He thought about climbing out of the window instead of going downstairs but decided it was more trouble than it was worth. She would be calling him all day at work. Then she'd have his sister call, and his sister would have his brother-in-law call. Then they'd have to have a family dinner at his sister's and discuss why he had "performed such and outrageously selfish stunt... and how worried mother had been all day," and inevitably the conversation would turn to him getting a job at his brother-in-law, Craig's, bank, working real hard and one day getting married to his girlfriend Lee, having their own house and children and—He laughed out loud, a high squeaky laugh that startled him. He felt his heart pounding against his chest; he got light-headed, dizzy. He thought he might be having a heart attack. He had read an article about a 35-year-old man whose heart had exploded in his chest for no apparent reason just two weeks prior, and he was 36. He sat on the edge of the bed and dropped his head into his hands and rubbed the palms hard against his eyes. Geometric figures swirled, appeared and disappeared against a field of black. It was soothing. He felt as if he were floating, just drifting through some other distant, removed space. "Elder, breakfast is almost done." He opened his eyes. His vision blurred, he stared forward, unblinking. He looked to the window, sighed, and fell back onto the bed.

He didn't iron his clothes, shave or shower that day. He brushed his teeth, dressed, and went downstairs. He noticed the startled expression on his mother's face but it seemed to be a stranger's face, a doll's face, unreal and not directed at him. He muttered something about not having time to eat, going to work early. His mother's voice and the gritty sound of her house shoes on the linoleum floor droned in his head like traffic in the distance. He walked through a tunnel across the kitchen, the back door the only clear object in his field of vision. "Elder you can't..." was all he heard before he closed the door. He staggered down the driveway to the sidewalk rubbing his temples and sighing a deep heavy sigh.

It was after he returned home that night, smelling of smoke and alcohol, confronted by his wild-eyed mother, still in her housecoat, his sister and brother-in-law, and a barrage of questions inquiring why he had called his job and fiancée and quit them both, that he smiled his crooked smile at them, stumbled up the stairs and into his room and discovered the piece of himself lying in his bed.

Elder looked at himself in the mirror. His skin was pasty and thin. The bristly growth of a three-day beard clung to his face like sand on a wet beach ball; dark semi-circles sagged beneath his eyes. He rubbed his hand across his face; he could see the white glow of the fluorescent bulb above the sink through his hand. He chuckled to himself and stepped back from the mirror to get a better look at the rest of his body. His stomach was sunken in and his ribs poked slightly through his skin. He looked at his face in the mirror again. He smiled at himself and wiped away a tear as it slid down his cheek.

On the way out Elder stopped at the kitchen door. He turned back around and walked to the kitchen table where his mother and sister sat with his flickering image. He kissed them both on the cheek and said goodbye. The two women continued to stare after him as he walked out the door and watched through the window on the door as he faded into the haze of the cold night.

In the pond at the park a lone duck floated in lazy circles upon the dark water. Elder sat next to himself, lit a cigarette, offered one to the wavering shadow who stared silent, motionless out into the trees beyond the pond. The image did not move. Elder shrugged and watched the duck. A strong breeze began to blow and it got colder. Elder heard the breeze blowing but didn't feel it. He laughed out loud. "You see buddy," he said, turning to the image on the bench, "intangibility is the best defense against your environment." He stood up, took a final drag from his cigarette, tossed it on the ground and crushed it under his foot. He stared at the phantom on the bench and smiled. "Better than a novel or a painting any day," he said, nodding. He left the bench and walked to a small clearing and lay on the ground with his head resting in the crook of his elbow. The wind blew from behind him and he watched with a disinterested calmness as the particles of his coat, pants and shoes blew away from him in small clumps and danced a whirling ballet with the wind. He held up his right hand and watched as the tips of his fingers slowly dissipated and floated away. Blowing constant in its path across North America, the wind was steady and cold, its current purposeful in its course. Elder smiled, laid his head back in the crook of his elbow and closed his eyes.

And to Think I Saw It on Broadway

I could hear nothing above the screams.

Below me panic spread like floodwaters. People ran, frenzied, directionless, nowhere. There was no escape. There was no-thing to escape from. Fear breed with rodent-like celerity. I watched, and it took all the strength in me not to jump down from my balcony and join in the chaos. There was something alluring about it, something almost sensual, promising. That fearful compulsion to jump from high places into a spiraling free-fall. I strained to see Lenore through the flames and smoke; I hoped she had gotten out of her apartment building before the riots began. Rolling below me was an orgy of agony. People stampeded in and out of buildings, they looted stores and houses. They filled their sacks, cars, and trucks with computers, TVs, video games, jewelry, satellite dishes, cell phones, tablets, robot vacuum cleaners, DVDs and players, sports teams apparel, greeting cards, fast food, piles of clothes, cosmetics, lawn furniture, and a thousand other things so necessary to their survival. They defended their possessions fiercely with guns, clubs, and fists. Then, when they were sure it was safe, they threw their booty away in a disenchanted fury and rushed to gather more of the same. They pushed, pulled, clawed, lashed, and stomped over others. I watched an elderly man and woman scratch and claw at one another, fighting for a digital clock radio that was flung out of the second story window of an apartment building and floated, curiously, above them, just out of reach. People ripped the clothes from their bodies and flagellated themselves with the steel belts from radial tires. I watched as some assumed the lotus position, doused themselves in gasoline and tried to light themselves on fire, but the fumes would not ignite so they only suffocated within a thick, black, oily cloud of smoke. Others crawled across the cement and broken glass on their knees crying and cursing, lamenting through prayer as they blew themselves up with pipe bombs and vests of C4. Still others marched up and down the street, some of them carried signs in protest against the madness: HEGEL LIED, THE END IS REVERED, BOYCOTT JOE'S. I climbed from my balcony to a tree below me. I stood upon what was left of an old tree house, and tried to form an explanation for all the madness below me, a unified theory of cause and effect. History demands explanations. A blue rhinoceros slammed into the trunk of the tree and my thoughts scattered as I groped and fumbled to regain my balance, but I fell down on the platform and split open my forehead. I tried to remember what I was doing, but my thoughts only came to me in fragments.

As I lay there, blood trickling in my eyes, in a reverie of yearning for Lenore, I saw, on top of some tall buildings made of glass and steel, a group of ruddy-faced men in finely-tailored, expensive black suits. One of the men threw white, blue, and red confetti off the building; the others stood on the edge, looking down, and waving conductor's batons, whistling The William Tell Overture. In another building, a single-level perfectly rectangular structure, I saw a pale man in a white lab coat peeking from behind the blinds with a clipboard and a pen. He would peek his large round head out from behind the blinds, write something then disappear only to emerge again in a few minutes to write down something else. The noise was growing to a deafening pitch. I began to get dizzy.

Yet something didn't feel quite right about it all.

I closed my eyes and I thought about Lenore. I thought I could hear her misty voice carried over the noise of the chaos like ashes taken by a strong breeze over a meadow of lilies of the valley. I strained to hear but the sound faded into static. I tried to picture her face, the line of her nose, the curve of her eyelashes, the hue of her lips but the image would fade, a tiny dot disappearing into a field of darkness like the signal from an old television.

Below me I heard gunshots. I crawled to the edge of my perch and saw soldiers in dark green uniforms shooting the people running directionless, and nowhere; then from a different direction more soldiers came, but they were dressed in black and they shot at the other soldiers, and then other soldiers from other directions came, some dressed in white, some in red, some in brown, and they all started shooting at each other. Then more and more came dressed in different colors until the colors faded together and every soldier was shooting at every other soldier and they were all dying. I stared, fascinated and appalled as blood sprayed the city's walls like obscene graffiti.

I watched as a cardinal, a bishop, and two priests frantically rushed in and out of St. Francis of Assisi church carrying their gold, holy objects, and loading them into a van driven by a Capuchin monkey wearing a tie-dye t-shirt with all the colors of the light spectrum. I watched as a group of donnish-looking men, thin, bespectacled, and wearing corduroy and tweed jackets surrounded them and filled them with bullets. The cardinal and the bishop fell to the ground, their bodies flailing as if they were having epileptic seizures, their blood, white thick curds of gelatinous mass, splashed against the walls of the church. As the priests were shot they popped and floated away on the wind like deflated balloons. One of the men yelled "Save the monkey, Save the monkey!" The monkey, barely escaping, as the van exploded in a ball of fire, at the same time consuming the donnish men in its wake, ran, chattering loudly, flipping the burning men, the bird, and disappeared into the chaos.

I watched as a group of children bludgeoned with nails stuck in boards some teachers sitting in protest against the madness. The teachers sat with their backs turned toward the chaos in the street, and each one alternately covered his or her eyes, mouth and ears. I watched as their blood, clear as water, splattered against the walls of the Ministry of Education, and it melted into puddles of clear liquid that was soon evaporated by the heat of the chaos behind them. The children danced the tango and composed poetry.

Again I felt the urge to jump off my perch and into the fracas. I stood up, yelled like a victorious Super Bowl quarterback and positioned myself on the edge of my perch when I saw a curious sight. One of the ruddy-faced men in the finely-fashioned, expensive black suits was standing behind a television camera pointed at the streets. I looked around and I saw that all the televisions, in all the store fronts still left intact, in all the houses and all the apartments, all the hospitals and schools, all the police stations and prisons, in the capital and in the mint, in the broadcast buildings and publishing houses, churches, synagogues, and mosques, were showing the chaos below me. And hundreds, thousands, hundreds of thousands of people stopped whatever they were doing. They stopped their directionless running, they stopped their self-flagellation, their looting, their buying, their killing, their dying, whatever they were doing, they stopped and watched, transfixed, the chaos on whatever television they were closest to. I watched children grab their parents, women begin to cry, and men hang their heads in silence. "I feel so sorry for those people, I'm so glad we don't live there," I heard a woman say. There was a murmur of agreement from the crowds, then a moment of silence. "To hell with them. Let 'em kill themselves, they're all crazy anyways," her husband shouted. "Yeah!" a cheer exploded from the multitude and they all continued to do what they had been doing.

I cheered with them and wished that Lenore had been at my side, for I knew she would have cheered too. I ached for her. It was painful to be alone.

From the rectangular building the pale man in the lab coat busted out of the doors. He was yelling and waving a huge piece of paper with mathematical formulas, diagrams, schematics, angles, circles and parallelograms scribbled across both the front and the back. He jumped up on a copper statue of an Indian with a tomahawk, feathered headdress, and bow and arrow triumphantly standing over a dead buffalo. The man mounted the buffalo, started pointing to the hieroglyphics on the paper, and talking with a feverish gusto. Several people stopped to listen to him, but no one could understand what he was saying and the noise of the mayhem was beginning to drown him out completely. They looked at one another, shrugged, and began to wander off. Some laughed at him, some sneered him and called him a fanatic and spit at him. He jumped off the statue, his eyes wide and red, spittle foaming and flying from his mouth. He stomped around the statue yelling, grasping the paper in his hand, raising it above his head, and shaking his fist. He lunged at several people, thrusting the paper in their faces. Most people ignored him, except for a big man with a broken limb from an apple tree in his hands, which he shoved into the pale man's chest. The pale man fell to the ground; the apple tree limb blossomed flowers. Above, one of the ruddy-faced men erupted into laughter and began throwing coins onto the street.

Suddenly, I had the feeling that none of this was important or serious. As if we were trapped in a hall of mirrors and the events were a series of reflections refracting, perpetually back and forth. An elaborate production played out on a giant stage, none of it amounting to anything but what it was at this precise moment, forever. All of us necessary parts in an unnecessary machine. This idea calmed me down, and I sat and watched the show below me as if I were watching a fireworks display. The fires, the explosions, and screams seemed merely the soundtrack to a 21st-century 4th of July premier, spectacular extravaganza. I started to laugh and I felt like dancing to the music of the night when I was knocked out of my reverie by a silver dollar that flew out of the air and smacked me in the eye. I have still not regained sight in my right eye from that. The wound was real. I held my bloody face, and folded into the fetal position on my platform above the chaos.

On the roof of another building I saw a long line of strange, little, bony, brown-skinned people, alien-like, in front of another of the ruddy-faced men. He was handing out pennies to the people, and each one graciously bowed and kissed the man's hand after he gave them one. One tiny man tapped the ruddy-faced man on his belly then pointed to the ruddy-faced man's pocket. A roll of one hundred dollar bills was falling out. The ruddy-faced man patted the tiny brown-skinned man's head and gave him an extra penny. The next man in line refused his penny and pointed to the ruddy-faced man's pocket, requesting one of the bills. The ruddy-faced man smiled, shook his head, and gave the man three pennies. The man refused and adamantly pointed at the bills. The ruddy-faced man frowned, shook his head and motioned for the little man to leave. The little man jumped at the ruddy-faced man and began clawing at his pocket. The ruddy-faced man screamed and several men and women dressed in red, white, and blue, toting rifles, knives, chains, crosses, and rage clambered, insect-like, up the walls of the building, grabbed and beat the little man and threw him off the side of the roof. The little brown body smashed through the windshield of a fully loaded, dual air-bagged, rearview camera-equipped, acoustic-laminated windshield, triple-shielded inlaid-protected, noise reduction dash-insulated onboard STAR GPS-installed SUV. Another group of people surrounded the SUV, took pictures of the image with their cell phones and texted the pictures back and forth to one another with captions like, terrible, horrible, appalling. Then, staring unwaveringly at their phones, they walked away in the different directions they had come from.

Then I caught a curious sight out of the corner of my eye. At the edge of the city I saw several hundred people surreptitiously entering the mouth of a cave. They were entering single file and turning around nervously as if to make sure no one was following them. They were escaping! I knew this for certain. Hope filled my chest. I thought Lenore would surely be there. She was that type. She would not have sat and cheered with me. What a fool I had been to think that. She was smart. She would be away from the pandemonium, seeking peace, seeking solace. I leapt down from my perch and ran to where the deserters were. A group of men stopped me before I reached the line. "Who is the son of the king and the muse?" one of them asked me. "Orpheus, of course," I said, and they let me pass.

There was a long tunnel we all walked through that descended deeper into the earth. Eventually, the tunnel entered into a vast cavern, the top of which I couldn't see because it disappeared into darkness. The rest of the cavern was filled with light and music, and songs and laughter. Carved into the walls were small compartments and inside of them people were sleeping, reading, making love, eating or just looking out at the merriment around them. There was an orchestra that had to rival any that could have been imagined in any heaven. There was every kind of instrument that I had ever seen: lyres to didgeridoos, tubas, guitars, synthesizers, washboards, and jugs, DJs, calliopes, I could go on. Other walls were painted with the most beautiful paintings in all styles from every era. Solitary women and men sat off from the rest of the people writing in notebooks or typing on laptops. Strange symbols and words were written upon some of the walls, and I swear I think I saw Michael Rockefeller with a bone through his nose mingling amongst the crowd sipping on a sour apple martini. Every once in a while, a small stone would fall from above. Each time a stone hit the ground the entire population of the cavern would chant in unison, "Unite, Unite, Unite against the top," then they would go back to what they had been doing. I felt peaceful as I walked around the cavern, but I still missed Lenore. I ate, drank, and engaged in intellectual conversations about what should be done about the bedlam above, but all the while watching for Lenore. A man that uncannily looked like Gandhi, drinking a cosmopolitan, came up to me as I stared up into the darkness of the cavern's ceiling, listening to the noise from above. "We will be safe down here, we will be safe, Unite," he said. I tried to ask him if he had seen Lenore, but he only smiled at me and repeated what he had said, then walked away. I watched as he walked and a huge chunk of earth fell from above and crushed his skull. He fell to the ground limp, but still held onto his drink. "Unite, Unite...," the others cried. More chunks began to fall, and each time they were bigger. I saw four more people fall, crushed beneath stones. I yelled out Lenore's name, but the only response I got was: "Unite, Unite, Unite..." I left the cavern and did not look back as I ran through the tunnel. Then I left the cave I looked back and the opening collapsed.

I returned to my perch. I could hear nothing above the screams. Below me panic spread like floodwaters. People ran, frenzied, directionless, nowhere. There was no escape. There was no-thing to escape from. Fear bred with rodent-like celerity. I watched, and it took all the strength in me not to jump down from my perch and join in the chaos; there was something alluring about it, something almost sensual, promising. That fearful compulsion to jump from high places into a spiraling freefall. I strained to see Lenore through the flames and smoke; I hoped she had gotten out of her apartment building before the riots began. Rolling below me was an orgy of agony. People stampeded in and out of buildings, they looted stores and houses then threw their booty away in a fury. They pushed, pulled, clawed, lashed out, and stomped over one another. I could hear nothing above the screams. Below me panic spread like floodwaters. People ran, frenzied, directionless, nowhere. There was no escape. There was no-thing to escape from...

Rain, Not Tears upon my Face

He feels it. He feels it spread like an army of insects up from his balls to his perineum, up the small of his back, through his spine, across his shoulders, around his neck until it explodes in his hypothalamus, flooding the rest of his body with that warm liquid feeling as if he were floating in a hot bath. You watch it. You recognize it. What is it? The way her red dress clings to her hips and hugs her flesh like a second skin? The lithe contours of her legs as they flow from thigh to calf to ankle? Everyone can tell even though he tries to hide it. His eyes gloss over and the corners of his lips turn up slightly. He looks high, or like a kid caught with his hands in his pants. He glows. He glows like the first star seen in a mid-summer night sky. And he is that star tonight. Tonight is his. But, it passes as soon as she passes. He wipes the corner of his mouth with his napkin and cracks a silly joke to regain his composure. Everyone laughs. He readjusts himself underneath the table. You put your hand on top of his, caressing it with your thumb, and laugh too.

Smiling that groin twitching, seraphic smile, a smile as perfect as a Michelangelo sculpture, he pours another round for the table. Pinot

Grigio. He watched that movie four times and read a book about wine. He is proud of his oenological knowledge now. He pours the wine and clicks the top of all four of the glasses with the bottle neck. For what? What is the click for? Then, of course, yes, the toast to beauty again. You wonder if he is toasting the beauty that just walked by, or the beauty of the softness of what's her name's vulva as his hand glided softly and slowly across it and his finger so nimbly slipped inside of her pussy? Or is he toasting the beautiful roundness of her ass as it thrusted against his pelvis, and the high-pitched little squeaks that escaped from her throat, like the whistle of steam from a teakettle? Maybe it is the beauty of her tits as his tongue outlined the soft areolas and so gingerly flicked each nipple? You wonder if he still thinks the prominence of your cheeks is beautiful.

Tito. His lips are shaped like the sound of his name.

It's raining outside. Storefront neon and headlights glow like will-o-the-wisp through the plate glass window of the restaurant. Thin rivulets of rain twist down the glass like transparent crystal snakes. Did he tell her the shape of her body reminds him of the way the rain falls against the window? You heard him say that about a woman once. Did she have those gentle serpentine curves? Did she move like Salome? Did she tickle his nuts with an owl feather, like that redhead in that video he thinks he's being so sly watching when you're not at home? Did she pitch his head into a tumult? Yes, Tito, here's to beauty.

The paisley design in the hallway carpet is nice, it's subtle. But, the red is too dark, too maroon, it looks like blood. Copies of copies of Renaissance paintings in mock baroque frames and mirrors line the walls. He loves it though. He's sitting back at that table soaking in all this... luxuriousness? He loves the big band thing going on, ice sculptures and champagne fountains, pretty tuxedoed waiters with complexions like mannequins. He deserves to be here. He's sitting there drinking up the abundant compliments about his play. Did she tell him he should try the salmon here?

A man walks alongside of you to the restroom. He wears a suit like the suits your father used to buy at Sears. The bathroom is clean, anyway. The attendant is handsome with stark hazel eyes, pretty lips, and a nice smile. Black pants, white shirt, and a black vest. There is lint all over the back of his vest. He has the expression of a cat in a cage at an animal shelter. Another guy at the urinal has the same pair of slacks Tito bought in Houston last year. You wonder, did she go down on him in an elevator? He liked it so much in Houston when you did it, did he bring the game home with him? The attendant hands you a towel, white terry cloth, partially wet, then a bottle of lotion. The lotion feels good. He takes the three dollars you offer him and puts them in a carafe with a few quarters in it. His fingertips are calloused; he's probably a musician hoping his music will rescue him from handing out mints and cologne in a toilet. Maybe it'll happen. Tito wrote the play and got it produced in less than two years. Now he can afford to eat here, here in a place where they have ice-sculpture swans and a man in the bathroom to make you comfortable after a bowel movement. Here's to beauty.

The waiter brings another bottle of wine, Pinot. Tito forgoes a toast. He tells the story about meeting August Wilson during grad school. Everyone has heard the story, but they smile and nod like good friends do. You look at him; you notice the lines around his eyes for the first time. You think it makes him look... more... mature. You want to share this moment with him, you want to ask him if he notices the way the rain falls against the window tonight. It is serpentine, a myriad of thin, winding, currents weaving the reflection of light into a pattern of paisley, connecting, pooling in the sill of the window, flowing in a tiny waterfall over the edge and disseminating into the crevices of cement swelled with the green life of plants struggling through the cracks. But, the band has just started up a Glenn Miller number, and you don't want to disturb him with silly little things. He wants to dance. You follow him to the floor, hand in hand smiling all the way.

Hail to the Bus Driver, Bus Driver-Man

His breath slid from his mouth and nose in clouds of smoky steam. He bounced up and down, shifting his weight from foot to foot, hugging himself, patting and rubbing his arms. The bright yellow glow of the street lamp above him flickered off; a moment later it fluttered back on casting a dim pink halo of light into the surrounding night air. He pulled his shirt sleeve up to look at his watch. A snowflake landed on the glass face and melted. It was 9:38. The bus was late. He stared down the deserted hall of the downtown street. A silvery haze floated around the bright orbs of the other streetlamps that lined the dark street; he watched as snowflakes drifted into and out of the light.

"Damn, it's freezing out here," he whispered, buttoned the top button of his shirt and lifted the collar.

If it hadn't been for that jerk Carl I wouldn't be freezing my ass off right now, he thought. It had been the third time this month that Carl had left without completing the data reports and when someone in his department didn't do their work it was up to him to finish it. It wasn't hard work, but it was long, tedious, and Carl was careless in his calculations so it took him that much longer to complete a report.

The task of uncompleted reports always fell to him because he was the best at what they did. The variables of information they analyzed and compiled rarely escaped his attention. It was why he was team leader: he always noticed the things other people didn't.

He realized he had forgotten his coat when he had decided to leave. He tossed his tables and graphs into his desk drawer, saved his spreadsheets, turned off the monitor and ran to the elevator. He didn't realize he had left without it until he stopped running and the cold air leapt onto him like something alive. He had made it to the bus stop with three minutes to spare. But the bus was late. The snow began to fall harder.

I don't know if it's worth it, he thought. Everyday it's something new. Extra reports, can you take a look at this, can you crunch these numbers real quick, can you find last month's A-7 reports and blah, blah, blah. What the hell do I get? Caught in a snowstorm without a coat. Don't I know about this anymore. I have a life. I have plans for a future. I'm better than this.

He heard the low tone rumbling of shifting gears. He lifted his chin from his chest, folded his collar around his throat and looked down the street. The headlights from the bus shone a dull, hazy blue in the cold air and seemed to quiver through the falling snow. He watched, but they did not come any closer.

"Please don't be broken down, please, don't break down," he said, bouncing in place and rubbing his arms faster.

Then the bus advanced. Then stopped again. Then moved again. The man could see the inside lights of the bus flickering on and off. It took five full minutes from the time he saw it at the end of the block for it to reach his stop. The light flickered on as the door opened and a quick jet of warm air escaped out into the cold. He felt it for a quick moment and hurried to it.

"This thing's not gonna break down, is it?" he asked stepping into the bus and putting change into the meter.

The bus driver, a large moon-faced man with shiny, piggish eyes smiled at him.

"Figures, it didn't add up, you know?" the driver said to him.
The man looked at the driver, shrugged his shoulders and sighed. The

bus was empty so he took a seat in the middle. He could already feel the heat warming him.

Out of the corner of his eye, the driver looked up into the big rear-view and peered at the lone figure of the man sitting in the middle of the bus. He thought that there was something strange, something suspicious about the man. It wasn't the fact that he was out in a snowstorm without a coat, hat, gloves or anything else. It wasn't the way his high cheekbones hid his eyes in dark circles, or the way the right side of his lip pointed slightly upward giving his mouth a sort of wry snarl. It was the way his collar rode up on his neck, the thinness and length of his neck and how the vein in his neck had tightened when he first got on the bus and heard the code words. Figures, it didn't add up. It was the almost imperceptible reaction to the code words that alerted the driver to who he was dealing with. Sometimes it was a twitch of the eye, or they would scratch their ear or chin, or a muscle would spasm in their forearm, and then he would know. He would know that they had found him again.

He looked to the road. The snow had not yet begun to stick to the street, but an icy sheen captured the red and green reflections of traffic signals in a kaleidoscopic haze. The driver looked at the man again. That's one of them, he thought. I saw him staring at me at Walgreens earlier today. I saw him signaling the pharmacist while I waited in line to fill the prescription. I remember the dingy grayness of his shirt, the driver thought. They always try to dress down and fool people like they're regular people. They think that if they wear un-ironed, dingy white dress shirts and khaki slacks that they can hide out in the public and fit in. But I know, the driver thought, I know who they are. That's why I didn't fill the prescription. I noticed the communication. I'm aware of things other people don't notice. They're changing the medicine on me. He took a small brown medication bottle from his shirt pocket and looked at it. The bottle read Trifluoperazine, but he knew the pills that had been inside the bottle had actually been Sodium Pentothal. He knew his doctor would be angry if she knew he hadn't taken his medication for a whole week, but he knew that they had been substituting his meds with other dangerous and mind-controlling substances. Maybe she's in on their plan, he thought. I'll have to investigate that further if I get out of this situation alive. He tossed the bottle into the little plastic trash bag that hung from the knob for his headlights. He glanced again at the man. He was staring out of the window. If I can get him to turn his head, the driver thought, I could see the mole above his eye, they all have a mole above their left eye, it's how they identify each other.

"Starting to come down pretty hard, huh?' the driver said.

The man ignored him.

He knew the driver was only trying to be nice, but he was in no mood for chatting. He was tired, angry and he needed a drink. He stared out at the snow; it had started to fall in fat, heavy flakes that fell wet against the window and slid down leaving watery trails that blurred the world outside the bus. He slid a bit further down in his seat so the driver might get the hint to leave him alone. I can't even get a break on the bus, he thought. Can't people just shut up and leave each other alone sometimes. I just want to get home, get drunk and pass out. Forget about that idiot Carl, forget about accounts, forget about figures and numbers, forget about the whole damn world.

The bus stopped at a red light. He watched a small red car, wavering, blurry through the melting snow on the window, trying to pull away from the curb, but the tires were only spinning in the slushy snow that had started to accumulate on the street. Sucks to be you, but at least you got a car, buddy, he thought. I'm never going to get shit working in this place. I haven't had a raise in three years; I do twice as much work as everybody else and make half as much. Whatever. I just need a new job. Yeah, right, and when am I going to get time to look for one? I'm there 7 to 7 every day. Hell, I'll be lucky if I don't die there. Goddamn it, he thought, and tapped his forehead with the palm of his hand, I'm not going to have a coat in the frigging morning. The light in the bus flickered off for a brief second then came back on in a dim gray wash of light that cast both the driver and the man in shadow.

Maybe it isn't Sodium Pentothal, the driver thought, I would think it would make me feel different, more gregarious, less inhibited. Maybe it's nano-technology. I can feel it. Yeah, yeah that's it. That's what the bastards have done. There's nano particles, like a trillion microscopic aphids, rushing through my blood stream into my head, short-circuiting the bio-electrical signals between my synapses. Holy Christ I—horn blared. The driver looked up and saw the red light as the bus passed through it.

"Sorry about that," he said looking up into the rear at the man. "I was going too fast to stop in this weather, you know."

The man looked away from the window to the bus driver. He sighed and leaned his head back on the seat.

Focus, you need to pay attention, the driver thought. He slowed the bus down and turned the windshield wipers on high. Pools of water formed behind the blades and were flung off the window in a smooth arc. He could see the snow getting deeper on the street, but he didn't notice the man at the bus stop in the gray trench coat and the black Cossack cap stepping off the curb into a puddle of icy water trying to flag the bus down.

I have to remember to get avocados tomorrow, the driver thought.

This driver's a nimrod, the man thought; he just completely ignored that guy back there. Oh well, I don't care. I just want to get home. I'm hungry. That left-over curry sounds great right now. Oh damn, that's right I ate it after I got back from the bar last night. I don't have shit else, either. I could call Todd and ask if he wanted to go out and eat, but I'm broke, and he never has money. Damn I'm sick of this. Sick, sick, sick.

He cupped his hands and rubbed them over his forehead to the back of his head, rested his head in the palms of his hands for a quick moment then massaged his temples and sighed again. The bus driver was looking at him in the rear-view mirror. The man looked back for a quick moment, shook his head, then turned and stared out the window again.

The driver watched the man moving his hands over his head. A signal? he thought. Is he signaling somebody? Do I have a tail? He bent over to look out the top of the bus window at the surrounding buildings trying to see if he could spot someone in a window or on a rooftop. He glanced in his side-view mirrors. There were no cars behind them and no one was on the streets. There was just the snow that was beginning to fall heavier. What the hell is he doing? Is he steeling himself for a physical assault? The light in the bus flickered on bright again then shut off. The driver pulled out a pocket knife, clicked opened the four-inch blade and set it across his lap. The man looked at the bus driver, and the driver looked back at him through the rear-view mirror. The bus engine stuttered and the bus lunged forward.

Great, the man thought, the damn bus is going to break down. A perfect coda for a shit song of a day. He slid down into his seat. I hate my job. There's so many better things I could be doing. I hate the people at that place. My talent is wasted there. I'm so much better than all those mediocre shits. They hired me because I'm the one who could get things done. I'm the one who notices the small important stuff that no one else notices, and fixes it. That firm would be nothing without me. I'm the one that keeps us out of trouble. It's time they started to appreciate me. If I walked out on them tomorrow they'd be screwed. I'm young, smart, and I have an unlimited future in front of me. It's time I took control of that future. I determine my own destiny. He took out his phone and dialed his girlfriend's number. He felt better with his new conviction and he wanted to share his optimism with her. The light in the bus flickered on again then shut off. The man remembered this was the night his girlfriend liked to stay in and watch her favorite TV programs. He hung up the phone and put it back in his pocket. He watched the snow start to stick to the window. I hate this damn snowy, cold state, he thought.

The driver glanced back and forth from the man to the road. He saw the light from the man's cell phone. He's activating them, the bastard is activating them right now, he thought. A beady film of sweat popped out on his forehead, he ran the back of his hand across his brow and wiped the wetness on his pants. A small dark green spot stained his light green pants. He clutched the knife. There's not a thing I can do. It'll be a matter of hours before my whole system is overrun. Dear God, they can use me for anything they want. He slowed the bus down and looked up into the rearview mirror. The man was staring out of the window again. Fuck you, and your smugness, the driver thought, how callous are these people. He sits there as if nothing in the world is wrong. I should just rush back there and take him out with the knife. That would surprise his cocky ass. If I stabbed him straight in his jugular vein, watched him suffocate on his own blood. He could have a gun though. He'd shoot me before I could get close enough. I just have to get away. I could jump out of the bus and let it crash. I could speed it up, open the door, jump out and run. The worst that'll probably happen is a broken arm. No biggie. He passed another rider at another stop, and the man looked toward him. Shit, the driver thought, he may be on to me, and he sped up the bus.

The driver began to scratch his forehead and temples; he ran his fingers under the soft bags beneath his eyes and felt the glands in his neck. Oh sweet Christ, he thought, and stuck his right pinky finger in his nose. He looked at the finger to see if he caught any nano-particles. He could feel them traveling beneath his skin to his liver and kidney, his spleen, his lungs and his heart. He began to scratch is forearms, neck and shoulders. He pressed the gas and the bus sped up a bit.

You nasty bastard, the man whispered, when he saw the driver stick his finger in his nose. Then he's going to wipe it on his arm, he thought. Sick ass man, he said under his breath. Why does my life have to be filled with all the dumb-asses? He thought. Damn, I just want to get off this bus and get home. I don't even need to eat. I got that half bottle of gin; I'll take a Xanax and fall out in front of the tube. The light above him flickered on and stayed on. It was dimmer and cast a pinkish haze above him. He scratched his eyelid, and stared out into the wet night. The snow was falling heavier and he could not see beyond the white static haze.

I have to do it, the driver thought. There's no other recourse. I have the code words. The people of the federation will know how to get these things out of me. I know the right words to get into the underground. I've got to jump off, find a pay phone, dial the code numbers and tell them the right words. If I'm fast enough, he'll never know what I'm doing. Snow settled heavy on the bus window and the wipers moved slow and laboriously to toss the wet piles off the window. He could see the dim wavering halo of a green light in the distance. He looked back at the man through the rearview mirror. I'm breaking you buddy, he thought, and looked back at the road. I'm getting out of here. No matter what, I'm getting out of here. He pressed his foot against the gas pedal and started to depress it. The bus sped up.

The man's phone rang and he answered it.

"What's up, man? the voice on the other end said.

"On the bus heading home, man. What's up?" the man said.

"Where the bus at?"

"Colfax and Fillmore, why?"

"Get off at that 7-11 on Ogden and I'll pick you. It's hump day, bro, we'll go to the Satire and have some brews, bro."

"I don't have any money", the man said.

"I won the football pool at work, dawg. I got your back"

"Cool, I'll get off at the next stop."

The man closed his phone and put it back in his pocket. He reached up and pulled the wire to signal a stop. The bus driver jumped and looked back at the man. The ding of the bell reverberated long in the empty bus.

"Next stop, please," the man said.

The driver continued to look back and forth from the man to the road. He sped the bus up, shifted in his seat, unbuckled his belt and opened the front door.

The man stood up and waited at the back door. He watched the driver looking back and forth from him to the road. Man, this guy is goofy, he thought. He could see his stop approaching but the driver didn't seem as if he was going to slow down. He pulled the wire three more times.

"Yo, man, I want to get off at the next stop.

The driver stared at the man through his rearview mirror.

"It's not adding up, right? Figures it's not adding up," the driver said almost yelling.

"What? Listen, man, I got no clue what you're talking about but are you gonna slow down so I can get off?"

The driver continued to stare at the man, his eyes began to water and his breath came in short rasps. The man raised his arms and shrugged. That's it, the driver thought. That's the sign I wanted to see. The man had surrendered and given up his mission. I dodged a bullet the driver thought. He could feel the deactivated nannites shut down and exude from the pores of his skin with his sweat. He slammed on the brakes and the tail-end of the bus slid to the right and hit the curb. The man fell forward against the glass door then tripped backwards and fell on his butt.

"What the fuck, man? Are you drunk or something?" he yelled.

The driver scooted back in his seat and straightened his posture. He turned in his seat and looked back at the man. He raised his hand to his forehead and saluted, then he opened the door.

"Have a good night, sir, and watch your step," he said, sitting back in his seat.

He rubbed his belly. No more avocados, he whispered. No more avocados on my salads. I'm gaining too much weight.

The man jumped out of the bus and gave the driver the finger. He pulled his collar tight around his neck as he stood under the bright fluorescent glow of the 7-11 awning. He watched his friend's Escort slide into the parking lot. The car slid past him a few feet and came to a stop as it bumped into a parking block. The man smiled and walked to the car. Alright, he thought. Finally I get a break tonight. Now I just need some nachos and some brews and everything will be right with the world.

Strangers

I met her at Milton's.

I was the only one in the restaurant, but there were seven or eight people in the lounge listening to jazz. The two sections are separated by a row of yellowed, chipped, and cracked plaster Corinthian style columns and thick, velvet maroon curtains. The sound of Myra and Abe drifted delicately through the cracks between the curtains on a thin cloud of gray smoke. They were the house band and performed every night as an opening act. Myra Reed was a big, loud woman with a small boil on the left side of her nose that she colored with an eyebrow pencil to make it look like a beauty mark. She was the singer, and she would one day be incarcerated for burning a boyfriend and another woman in the bed she found them together. Abraham Henderson was the piano player. He was a small, thin man with a hunchback that twisted his spine so it looked like he was always about to fall over. Abe had about eight teeth in his mouth; he would eventually die of colon cancer. They were very good, and on any other night I would have been in the lounge drinking scotch, smoking cigarettes, and listening to the music. They were playing an eerie, surreal rendition of "Strange Fruit." But that night I felt detached, removed, lonely. I was half-ass reading a tattered old copy of Borges' *Everything and Nothing*, writing ideas in my notebook for the book I would never write, drinking a beer, picking at a burrito, and watching the images from the news on the muted TV above the bar. Apparently a new strain of some deadly disease was ravaging the population of some poor African country.

Jean, a new waitress, was a woman I had gone to high school with; she looked faded, lonely and wrecked now. That the once untouchable princess, whose incredible thick thighs and pouty lips had been the subject of countless sessions of nocturnal self-abuse, was slinging hash in a downtown dive and serving me gave me a perverse sense of satisfaction. I thought about all the others that had been in her little circle of elite and hoped they too had encountered similar fates. But the real irony of the situation was that I was in a downtown dive, coming from a job that I detested—that allowed me to exist in the troughs of mediocrity—harboring twenty years of juvenile self-pity and still feeling lustful for the woman. I would have been with her that night if she had wanted to: if both of us weren't wearing rings, if our acknowledgement of each other had been more than just cautious smiles, if the conversation we didn't have wouldn't have ended up being the same conversation we couldn't have had in high school, if I didn't have to actually touch her, if I didn't think she'd be thinking about her husband, and I'd be thinking about my wife, I think, and because of the cautious smiles, if all those things hadn't been obstacles, we could have been together that night. Maybe, too, if my staring at her like she was a dollop of sour cream for my burrito, had been more sincerely sensual and less stolid, we may have been together.

I took a bite of the burrito; it had turned cold. I read the last entry in my notebook before I closed it. It read:

I sometimes feel as if the world is surrounded by a thin transparent film, and outside this thin film is emptiness. And like a dark, living, gelatinous thing, it grows and pulsates against the thin film—some primeval invertebrate in the wake of orgasmic tremors—seeping through the tiny pores of the film and creating objects in the world. And I can sometimes feel the things around me disintegrating.

When I close my eyes I can see the walls of buildings surrendering to gravity in small chucks and gray dust, I can see the horizon and the sky dissolving like a slug in salt, and behind it is darkness... Nothing.

I scratched it out and crumpled up the page. Jean came by and asked if I needed another beer. I told her yes.

I had been there for two and a half hours. I didn't want to go home. I was comfortably and hypnotically insulated by a superlative buzz. My wife was home. And the obligation of acknowledgement between us seemed too overwhelming at the time. I love my wife. I do. It's just that numbness, somehow, through an unspoken mutual agreement, had supplanted any type of connubial sensitivity that we may have experienced in the past. I have tired of the redundancy of all my psychological and philosophical inquires of this state. People over time become different people, and sometimes those people are just too different for one another. And then a space is created. This space is as the sun, now. A permanent presence in our lives. A monument to the expected, inevitability of dissolution. The silence that filled the space between us would have been just too much to bear.

Veronica walked in and sat at the counter. I heard the click of her high-heeled shoes on the linoleum, and I looked up from my book. She carried a small black purse and wore a black spaghetti strap dress that stopped at mid-thigh and hugged her body like a wet t-shirt. She was sculptured, a figure skater's body with a set of long, legs that curved elegantly from her perfect round hips. She saw me and smiled; I averted my eyes, lowered my head, and picked up the book as she walked past my table. Then, without moving my head, I lifted my eyes and watched her slide onto a stool. As she sat down the hem of her dress moved up the curve of her thigh revealing the smooth flesh of her hip. I felt a wave of heat spread across my body. She quickly slid a hand under her hips and pulled the dress back over her thigh. She looked back over her shoulder; I pretended I was stretching my neck. I nodded my head in a disinterested way and turned back to the book. Peeking up again, I noticed how her hair—long, brown, and wavy with sandy blonde highlighted streaks—flowed over her exposed shoulders. "Do ya need anything else?" Jean said, standing in front of me blocking my view. She was looking down at me with her hand slung on her hip and a slightly exasperated expression on her face.

"No, just the beer you just asked me about," I said smiling. She took my burrito without asking, turned, and with less sway and more speed in her step, walked away.

I watched Veronica over the spine of my book. She sat at the counter with her legs crossed sipping a beer, from the bottle no less. Jean brought my beer, sat it down on the table with a thud and walked away without saying a word. Veronica turned around at the sound, flipped a long curl off her face, raised her eyebrows as if asking me what Jean's problem was, and smiled. I smiled back. With a sigh of accomplishment, I finished my beer in three gulps, as if that might have somehow made me attractive or proved that I was worthy of her full attention. Jean was there right away with another one. "Thanks," I said, "but I didn't—" "It's from her," she said, and cocked her head toward the counter. Veronica spun around on her stool, I held up the beer and said, "Thank you." She said "you're more than welcome," and we smiled at each other. There was an awkward moment of silence as we both waited to see who was going to take the next step. She must have seen the stupor that I felt. She must have noticed that my eyes had quit blinking and that my thin salamander smile had lasted a moment too long, and was starting to wane with a twitching in the corner of my mouth.

"What are you reading?" she asked. I snapped out of my trance feeling embarrassed and incompetent. I slowly raised the book in front of my face to show her the cover.

"Borges, oh yes," she said getting off the stool and coming over to the booth. She slipped in across from me and asked to see the book.

"You know Borges?" I asked.

"Yeah, I majored in English at Purdue, but I just sell insurance, now. Four years and seventy-thousand dollars later, all I do is scam the public," she said with a giggle. "What's your name?"

"Max," I said, "Max Alvarez. What's yours?"

"Veronica Swanson." She extended her hand across the table and I took it in mine. Her hand was soft and I held onto it for a moment even after we had lowered them to the table.

"So what do you do, Max?"

"I manage a computer store."

"Really?" she said.

We looked away from one another. Myra and Abe started a new song.

"Yep. It's not much, but it pays the bills."

She nodded her head. We looked at each other again and she erupted with laughter. I immediately felt uncomfortably self-conscious and thought she was laughing at me for some reason. I was about to defend myself when I guess she noticed the expression on my face.

"I'm sorry," she said through a snicker, "but I don't think it can be any more obvious that we both hate our jobs."

I chuckled and nodded. There was a welcoming sincerity to her frankness that made me like her, outside of just being overwhelmingly lustful for her. She was friendly and that was rare in my experience with people in general.

"Yes, well, I can honestly say it was not what I dreamed about being when I was a kid."

She giggled some more. "'ll tell you, Max," she said, "my work is so banal it should be made illegal for cruel and unusual punishment."

I laughed loudly and I saw Jean glare at us.

"Actually, insurance is such a scam it should be illegal. I get paid for telling lies. It's a bit depressing at times," she said. "But, yes, you're right, it does pay those bills."

She smiled at me. "Do you want another beer?" She asked.

"I'll get 'em," I said.

I walked over to the counter where Jean was sitting smoking a vapor cigarette and asked her for two more beers. She sort of twisted off the stool and held her arms close to her sides, so as not to let any part of her clothing or body touch me. "Excuse me," she said, and I backed up and let her pass. She disappeared behind the velvet curtain. I leaned against the counter and looked at Veronica over my shoulder; she was flipping through the pages of the book. I wondered what she wanted with me. I thought for a second she might be a hooker, and it irked me that I might seem that pathetic to her. I thought she might be gold-digging, but if she was, I figured she wasn't very good at it to try to work a slightly over-weight, frumpy middle-aged man dressed in Dockers and a sweaty dress shirt. Jean returned with the beers, "I'm closing the kitchen, you can go to the bar in the lounge if you want something else," she said and walked past me into the kitchen. I left a ten on the counter.

Myra and Abe had just finished their set when we went into the lounge. We sat at the bar silently sipping our drinks and eyeing the other people in the place. Members of the new band, Silent Rescue, were setting up their gear for their set. A few more people, mostly guys dressed like me in wrinkled dress shirts, ties hanging lopsided like nooses around unbuttoned collars and coats thrown over one shoulder had straggled in for their nightly after work therapy session. They would sit at the bar for the next three hours, their conversation taking its usual course in direct proportion with the amount of beers they drank: from their frustration with their inability to enter in to the upper echelon of inner-office politics, to stock options, to their aspirations and consequent failures of lodging themselves between the legs of their female co-workers. I turned and looked at Veronica's profile. She was captivatingly beautiful and I wondered why she was there at Milton's Paradise Lounge.

"So are you from Indiana?" I asked, trying to re-establish the comfortableness we had had in the restaurant.

"No, actually I'm from Pennsylvania. I got outta there right after graduation."

"So you live here now?"

"No, I live in Philly. I've been here for a week, training a new girl for the Denver branch. I leave to go back home tomorrow."

"How do you... how did you end up here?"

"Here as in this bar with you?"

"Yeah, I suppose so, in this place, with me."

"Tsh," a thin wispy sound like the sound of a match being extinguished in syrup, escaped from her mouth. "I don't know, really," she said, looking down at the bar and tracing the lip of her bottle with the tip of her finger. "I was supposed to meet Erica, the girl I've been training, at some nightclub up the street. I'm just in a hotel around the corner, and as I was walking there I just started feeling... I don't know... just... strange. You know? I just couldn't do it tonight, you know? All week I've been listening to this woman's inanities. All she talks about is men and clothes and cars and money and the mess other people are making of their lives. And I was going to this nightclub to meet her and two of her friends. I imagined that conversation and I just couldn't see myself doing it tonight, you know?"

"Yes I do," I said.

"So, I decided to stop in here for a couple drinks and call it a night. How did you end up down here?"

"This is my hangout. This place has a sort of instinctual moth to the flame attraction for the inconsolable. Which is why I can't understand why such a beautiful woman is here talking to me." She sat looking at me with her chin resting on her hand, and I watched with a knot in my stomach and warmth in my face as a smile appeared on her face. "Sorry," I said, "I don't mean to sound so negative."

"No, I understand," she said, "I know exactly what you mean. You just don't hear many people being that honest about it. I work and I smile at work, I act enthused when a supervisor is around, I don't complain about the long hours, the shitty pay, the lies I tell customers, or the crappy benefits. I smile in the faces of a thousand Erica's a day, my voice is continually pleasant, and I'm really good at what I do. And at the end of the day, after I neatly clean up my niche, I smile at all my co-workers on the way out of the office." She was quiet for a moment. Her eyes seemed to have narrowed to a tiny point and she stared at the bottles lined up in staggered rows behind the bar. I wanted to touch her. But, it had turned into something less sexual, less defined, but more urgent. "Then I'll meet my friends at the bar and drink white wine and rip my co-workers apart with sardonic witticisms until I'm safely insulated and can face going home alone to the Himalayan cat that I bought because she fit with my décor. Then I slip into bed and right before I fall asleep realize how much I really hate it all. And that doesn't even really explain the totality of it, you know?"

I don't remember exactly what I was thinking at that moment. I do remember feeling the weightlessness and warm flush of the alcohol, and resting both elbows on the bar as I leaned back on my stool, trying to keep my balance. I remember wanting to tell her I loved her.

"Listen, I'm sorry. I don't even know you and I'm telling you all this crap. I better go, it's getting late and—"

"No, no," I said, turning around to her and putting my hand on her arm. "Listen I'll buy you another one. You know, don't worry about that stuff, I understand, really. Don't go though, OK? I really need... I want you to stay. We can go somewhere else if you want, OK?"

She turned to me with eyes wide and watery. "I'm sorry," she said. I shook my head and caressed her arm. "Come on," I said grabbing her purse off the bar and handing it to her, "let's get out of here." She looked down at the finger on my left hand and I followed her gaze. The ring stood out with a brilliance, and I slid my hand underneath my thigh. Then she raised her eyes to my face and stared. I stared back into her eyes. A vacuum opened up around me and sucked away all the people and sound. The drumming of my heart was deafening. I felt a sense of vertigo and a sweltering heat. My mind fumbled for a way to escape this situation with the least amount of embarrassment. The urge to turn around and physically run away was my first coherent thought, but my legs felt as if they had no muscles. I sat immobilized, silent and foolishly staring at her.

"Do you mind if we just have a couple of drinks at the hotel?" she said.

The world returned with a shock, like a thermos of ice water poured down my back. Veronica grabbed her purse and got up. I was unsteady and I sort of stumbled off the stool and followed her outside, nervously fingering the ring.

We walked silently side by side up 16th street to the Holiday Inn. The streetlights and neon smeared the dark with a manila haze that caused the buildings to look like giant dioramas. It was getting cold so I gave her my jacket to put over her shoulders. She pulled it tight around herself and walked with quick short steps as if she were walking on ice. Her heels made loud clacking sounds on the concrete, and I looked around nervously to make sure no one I knew was around. I walked with my shoulders hunched and my hands jammed into my pant pockets. It was Thursday night and there were lots of people out already priming themselves for the weekend. The street shuttles passed by full with shadows standing rigid and close to one another. As we waited for a light to change, I heard a thin metal clicking sound like a handful of dimes tossed on a linoleum floor. I looked around and saw a guy with long graying hair, wearing a sleeveless t-shirt with a big black A in a circle on the front of it. He was terribly thin and his skin looked stretched and taut. His forehead, mottled with patches of brown spots, protruded from beneath his receding hairline like a decaying cantaloupe. His eyes were wide and vacant. He was singing, or rather a sort of low humming came out of his mouth from the back of his throat. He didn't have any teeth. He was strumming an out of tune electric guitar. He had the thing plugged into a battery-operated amplifier and I think he was trying to play some blues song, but I wasn't quite sure. He saw me and waved; I frowned and he winked at me. I wanted a drink. There was a liquor store catty-corner to us and I suggested we get a twelve pack of beer and take it up to her room. She agreed.

"Can I ask you something?" I said. She looked at me and nodded.

"Why me?" She was silent and kept walking then looked up at a streetlight and a piece of hair fell lightly across her face.

"Because you have a kind face. Because you were reading Borges, and because you looked as alone as I felt."

Veronica's room looked out onto the pool on the roof. I stood by the window and looked at the water. The pool caught the reflection of the huge electric letters of the building across the street; the Qwest logo wavered like a mirage. Just below I saw the flashing of red and blue lights and heard the screeching of an approaching siren.

She walked up behind me, placed her hand on my shoulder, handed me a beer and sat down on the foot of the bed. I sat across from her on the one chair that was in the room, hunched over with my arms resting on my knees.

"I want to apologize again for sort of freaking out in the bar. I'm so embarrassed, you just have no idea," she said.

"What are you apologizing for? You were just telling me how you feel, there's nothing wrong with that."

"I don't even know you, Max. Don't you think that's kinda strange?"

"Well, who knows anybody, really? Strangers are safer to talk to anyway. There's less, but more of a sincere commitment talking to a person you have no history with."

"I'm glad we came up here."

I scooted the chair closer to her, leaned over, and kissed her gently on the corner of her mouth. Her mouth was so soft. I let my lips rest against hers for a moment. I felt her skin warm against my nose and my chin; she leaned in closer and I moved my face slowly down the curve of her neck to her shoulders, caressing them with my cheek. She put her hands under my arms and gently pulled me forward off the chair onto the bed. I rolled over so that I was on my back, and she wrapped my arm around her and nestled her head on my shoulder. I closed my eyes and she unbuttoned the first three buttons of my shirt and slid her hand inside. Gently, lightly she swept her nails over my chest. I drew her closer to me and she kissed my neck so softly it sent chills down my back. I opened my eyes and she was leaning over me, resting her head on her hand.

"I haven't felt so... nice, so comfortable for so long," she said, then softly put her mouth against my neck. I squeezed her closer to me and she curled up against me, sliding her leg across my body. "I wouldn't care if the world disappeared right now, Max. I'm so tired of being alone, so tired of being angry, so tired of being afraid. This is right, Max. This is the only thing that's been right for... forever it seems. I don't know why all this is coming out with you, I don't even know you, but I trust you and I don't trust anything in this shit world, Max. It's a terrible world Max, but you're something good in it."

"Thanks, but I don't know. I think sometimes I'm what's wrong. I don't have the luxury to blame the world anymore. I have to consider, what if it's my inability to connect with it? The world has always been brutal and cruel, but what if it's my inability to create meaning from it that keeps it that way?"

"I don't understand," she said, and lifted her head up from my shoulder, resting her chin on my chest.

"I don't either, but I know this means something right now, lying here with you. I feel, so it must mean something right?" She kissed me, then laid her head on my chest.

We fell asleep.

I don't know what time it was when I woke up. It was still dark. I slid slowly out from underneath Veronica so I wouldn't wake her. I stood above her and stared at her for a moment. I debated for a moment whether to lie back down. I leaned over her and brushed my lips across her cheek. She was warm and soft and I whispered I love you to her. I looked around the room trying to burn as much of it in my memory as I could. There was a pen on the desk; it was a green Bic with Holiday Inn printed in white across its length, I picked it up and put it in my pocket and left.

The streets were clear and quiet, the noise from my footsteps echoed in the yellow neon haze. I stood at a corner waiting for the light to change. I saw the guitar player across the street rummaging through a trashcan. He saw me, and with a wide toothless grin he waved to me. Then he stood there for a long moment staring at me with his wide, hollow eyes. I winked at him; he frowned, turned and walked on down the street. As I walked to Milton's to get my car, I passed a newspaper box and read the headline: 12 Die in Suicide Bombing. I reached in my pocket to get my car keys and felt the pen. I rolled it back and forth between my fingers, took it out of my pocket and looked at it in the glow of a streetlamp. I got in my car, stuck the pen in my visor and drove away.

A Force of Nature

The jackhammer relaxed Herbert. The vibration shot through his body like the warm flush of narcotics. Wave after wave of force jolted his nerve endings, increased the synaptic firing of endorphic chemicals in his neural network, and charged him with a semi-euphoric sense of being. He increased the speed of the hammer; the vibration increased, his molars shook in his jaw. But he still felt teased. The jackhammer's recoil was unsophisticated, erratic, immature and premature, there was no way it would pitch him into the blue realm. There were too many factors missing. There was no conflict. Against the blacktop there was no struggle. The blacktop was too yielding, too soft. But, those rag-headed, sand-niggers shooting at him in the desert—the metallic, azure haze of gun smoke, the smell of dust, oil, gunpowder, and blood, the constant barrage of sound: explosions, cartridges being locked and loaded, the roar of tank engines and the helicopter blades slicing up the air, the screams and the curses and the hoorays of a hit—that was conflict. And that was the most important part.

His first and only battle in Desert Storm had been the high point of his life. It was an experience that over-shadowed everything else.

Before that, the closest he had ever come to feeling that kind of elation was when Mary Sue Tucker gave him head and swallowed while he watched *Full Metal Jacket* at the drive-in movie. In Iraq, it had been Trisha, his M-16, that put him over the edge. The recoil of the gun was soft and subtle, but it was steady and constant and pulsed through him like oil through a pipeline. The festive atmosphere and the warm thup, thup, thup of the machine gun's vibration pushed Herbert Hanson into a state of transcendence.

In the hospital, Pep Nelson, Herbert's comrade in arms, told him that he had seen a blue light envelope Herbert after he jumped onto the hood of a jeep and fired into the sand dunes around them. "You looked just like goddamn Stallone in *Rambo II*," Pep told him. Herbert remembered the world shifting into slow motion. He could see bullets as if they were leisurely floating by him on a current of air. Then the sound stopped and the surroundings melted into one vibrant color. A bright blue light, like he imagined heaven looked like when he was a kid, shimmered in front of him, and in a daze he walked into the light. He stepped into an empty blue space. He felt as if he had fallen into a cloudless sky, but at the same time was floating in a vast warm ocean. He felt a serenity that he had never experienced in his entire life, as if he were being born, dying, and screwing at the same time. Everything before that moment, he realized, had been frivolous, petty, banal, mundane—meaningless. In the blue place he felt alive; it throbbed around his flesh like a living thing. His nerve endings reached out for the blueness and sucked it into him like hungry roots drawing water from the earth. He felt as if he were part of a massive brain, a tiny cell in the brain of God.

A grenade landed in the back of the jeep. Pep Nelson lost both legs and Herbert Hanson lost his connection with the blue realm. He had felt an intense yearning, as if for an AWOL lover, and a profound detachment from everything since then. He once told a tarot card reader, while they engaged in coitus, about his experience. Afterwards, as she lay on her stomach, she told him that his vibrational field had probably somehow connected with the universal vibrational field, and he had experienced a oneness with the universe. Something about that had sounded right to him. He became intrigued, energized—hopeful by what she told him, and had her explain it to him throughout the night over and over as they engaged in sexual actions.

Herbert shut off the jackhammer and let it fall to the ground. He took a plastic, bullet-shaped container from this shirt pocket and snorted a blast of meth. He felt tired. The dope didn't even get him off anymore. He did it mainly to try to keep his vibrational field at an optimum level, just in case. In his truck, he put on the baseball cap with the American flag and the embroidered "Do It" sewed underneath the flag, popped the cap of a long-neck bud with his teeth, spun the wheels of the Dodge Ram, and sped out of the parking lot onto the highway.

A thick haze of smoke floated around the glow of the television mounted behind the bar. Lloyd, the bartender, put another shot of Wild Turkey and a Bud in front of Herbert without asking. Herbert nodded and drank from the beer. He listened to a reporter talking about Iraq. A sadness he felt molecularly spread through him. If the sniffle hadn't accompanied the tear that ran down his cheek he could have blamed it on the smoke, and Ben Johnson wouldn't have paid no mind to him. But, the sniffle turned Ben's attention away from Sally Greens chest like a shark attracted to the smell of blood. He turned and looked at Herbert then at the TV; he swung around on his stool with a wide yellow grin.

"Well my boy here gettin' sentimental on us, y'all."

Herbert closed his eyes and another tear slid down his cheek.

"Whooo boy, looka here! What's wrong honey britches? You worried them young boys over there gettin' hurt, ain't ya?"

Herbert opened his eyes. The sadness he had felt a moment before evaporated. A feeling of hot, navy-blue liquid seemed to shoot through his body. He grinned at Ben. "The Lord works in mysterious ways," he said, under his breath.

"Now Ben, you can't still be mad 'cause I banged your wife in the bathroom stall last month, now are ya?"

Ben whirled around and stood up. Herbert punched him in the nose. In slow motion, Herbert felt the flesh of Ben's nose spread across his knuckles and the cartilage beneath tear like plastic ripped from a frozen steak; the bone at the bridge of the nose crumbled. A scarlet spray squirted from Ben's face and hung like dust particles in the air. The rush of methamphetamine pulsed through Herbert as if he had shot it directly into his brain. He felt the vibration, and it was building. He smashed his right fist into the side of Ben's face. The contradiction of feeling, the soft malleability of the skin and the hardness of bone combining together against his fist in an oatmeal-like texture, was exquisite. A milky blueness entered his vision. He noticed the veins in his arms throbbing and popping to the surface of his skin. They had turned to a powder-blue color. He stood staring at his arms, feeling the vibration building in intensity. As the vibration built, Herbert grew larger and turned bluer. Ben lumbered toward him with a broken beer bottle. Herbert brought his fists together like a massive blue hammer, swung his arms in an inverse arch from his waist and connected with Ben's chin. He watched Ben, like a child, cruelly amazed as he tortured some small creature, fly off his feet and propel through the air, with a sort of odd acrobatic grace, five feet across the room. Ben's jaw dislocated from both sides of his face and his front teeth bit through the tip of his tongue. A thin rivulet of blood trickled from the corner of his mouth before he lost consciousness.

Herbert growled and flexed the growing muscles of his aqua-blue body. Sally Green screamed and Lloyd grabbed his shotgun. The last tatters of clothing fell from Herbert's body as he flexed again. Lloyd cocked the gun. Herbert whirled around and wrapped one mammoth blue hand around the double barrels, crushing them. He took the gun from the bartender's hand and smashed in the top of his skull with the butt. The vibration built and Herbert grew bigger and bluer. Then he smashed the bar and everything behind the bar, the tables, the electronic dartboards, the pool table, and the jukebox that had been playing Kris Kristofferson songs all night. He had grown too big to fit through the door so he smashed out a wall. After he turned the parking lot into a scrap metal dump, he bounded off down the street in great leaps, smashing everything in his way. He was connected again.

Everyone had a different story. Some say they had to call in the Marines to finally stop him. Some say a special FBI team headed by a man named Mulder came in and evaporated him with an invisible ray. Some say a little blonde girl in braids and a sucker stopped the monster in his tracks; he leaned down to accept the sucker, and the child kissed his hand then he just stopped smashing stuff and walked away into the night. Some say the earth itself opened up and swallowed the beast in a ring of fire. But Sally Green, who had become intrigued with the carnality of the carnage, followed the monster like a rat following the music of the piper. She said he just kept smashing stuff, growing bigger and bluer and smiling a ridiculously large smile until he just exploded like a giant sparkling 4th of July firework and disappeared in a blue smoke.

The Weight of Heaven

In April, on his birthday, Miles Nodin stopped functioning properly. It happened suddenly like the flash from a camera. Things just stopped making sense. It was that simple. He had been thinking about how he was going to make a killing at the roulette table in Blackhawk, when the world stopped making sense. He pulled his car onto the emergency lane off I-70 and Pecos, shut off the engine and the radio, rolled up his window, sat bolt upright in his seat and stared forward. He wasn't afraid; he just didn't know what to do. The road signs and signals, that moments ago, had directed his course, became incomprehensible geometric shapes with horizontal and vertical lines of different sizes and colors that seemed to be fashioned in a linear progressive pattern. Miles, turtle-like, retracted his neck and hunched his shoulders so he could peek out of the windows of the car. Things appeared to him. Explosions of multi-hued shapes crystallized in his sight. He watched the evolution of a cloud. There seemed no relation to the way it made his body feel and the urge to vocalize that feeling. "Uklok," rushed from his mouth, but it didn't feel right. So he stretched out his arms, pushed out his chest, and filled his cheeks with air, then began to slowly undulate and move his arms up and down in a wave-like fashion, and it felt right to him. The sound at the window caused him to smash his forehead against the steering wheel.

The highway patrol officer tapped on his window with the tip of a pen. Miles did not respond. He sat motionless and smiled at the officer, even when the officer threatened to take him to jail. The highway patrol man walked back to his squad car and radioed for backup. He waited in the car, his holster unclipped, until another highway patrol and two local police cars showed up. Five law officers surrounded the car, and the first patrolman, a jimmy in hand, approached Miles window again.

"Sir, if you don't open the door I will be forced to open it myself," the officer said.

Miles did not respond. The first officer shrugged, looked at the others as they pulled out their pistols and aimed them at Miles' car, and stuck the jimmy into the space between the window and the doorframe. He pulled the door open and pointed his gun at Miles, who did not respond and stared at him smiling.

"Sir," the officer said, stepping away from the car with his pistol at arms length, "please step out of the car. Miles remained motionless. Another officer, one of the locals, stepped toward the car and grabbed Miles by his collar and pulled him out of the car and pushed him onto the ground. The other four law officers ran over, and they all pointed their guns at Miles as he lay on the asphalt. One of the officers handcuffed him and pulled him to his feet by the collar of his suit coat. The first officer stood in front of him, and Miles nodded and smiled at him.

"What's your damn problem, nut bag? The first officer said to him.

Miles continued smiling and answered "Pqouknik." The other officers, their guns in hand, gathered in front of Miles and stared at him.

"Are you trying to be funny, freak?" one of them asked.

"Twemic," Miles said loudly and moved his body like Chubby Checker doing the twist.

The officer that pulled him up by his hair pushed him against the car.

"Keep still."

"Flupnu," Miles said still smiling.

"Do you think he's French or something?" one of the other local officers asked.

"French, huh?" said the officer who pushed Miles. "You know, I bet you're right. One of those sissy, terrorist-loving, commie faggots. You're right. I'd bet a hundred bucks, you're right."

He stepped up to Miles, grabbed him by the throat, and drew his face a quarter of an inch away from his own. Miles smiled.

"Is that it freak job? are you French, boy? A sissy wine-drinking faggot?"

"Phiop," Miles said, and a bit of spittle landed under the officers left eye.

The officer punched Miles in the stomach, and he fell to ground. He wasn't smiling anymore. He looked up at the officers with wide eyes, frightened.

"Guibdik!"

"Keep your trap shut," another officer said and kicked him in the thigh.

Miles stood up frowning and glaring at the officers and yelled "Oplifpe!"

"I'm tired of your smart mouth, frenchy. I think it's time you knew what it's like to be in America. Let's show him boys."

Francine, Miles' wife, was at a complete loss as to why her husband would be so contemptuous and disrespectful towards a group of peace officers. It was completely unlike him to do such a thing. He was an accountant for God's sake and did the taxes for doctors and lawyers. The police released him into her custody with the understanding that he was to remain under her supervision until he had to appear in court one month from the day of his release. She listened carefully and nodded enthusiastically. She gasped and was taken aback a bit when she saw Miles approaching from the corridor of jail cells. The purple bruises under his eyes, the hematoma on his forehead, and the swollen lip made him unrecognizable. Miles recognized her, raised his hand in greeting and smiled. The puffed-out, swollen lip made his smile look like an old-time photo of a sneering John Dillinger she had seen as a child. The arrogance and contempt that sneer represented had made her hate John Dillinger, and when she saw it on Miles, she frowned at him, folded her arms across her chest and impatiently tapped her right foot. Miles' smile faded and he walked the rest of the way with his head down.

Miles sat in the front seat of the car with his head out the window and a huge smile on his face. He craned his neck this way and that. His eyes darted to and fro. Francine, with her hands at 10 and 2 o'clock on the steering wheel, scolded him for acting the way he did with the peace officers. She asked him what he thought doctors Peterson, Ryans, and Richards would think when they found out their accountant had been arrested, and did he think that the Pinkerton, Oliphant, and Monroe law firm was still going to want to associate with an accountant with a criminal record, would they trust him not to become an embezzler after this incident? What was she going to tell her mother and father? Would the children become pariahs at school? How could he have been so thoughtless? Miles turned to her, his purple face beaming, he smiled then stuck his head back outside the window.

Francine sat on the veranda talking on the phone to her sister, Verna. She looked out at Miles, with that silly smile on his face, just drifting in the pool on his back as if he didn't have a care in the world.

"Yes, the bruises have disappeared, but he still insists on being uncooperative. He just walks around here making silly sounds with that intolerable smile on his face. It's infuriating, Verna."

Miles floated in the pool with his arms and legs sprawled out wide. He looked like an enormous snowflake, weightless and airy. He stared up at the vast expanse of the sky, he felt as if his body had disappeared and that the only thing that existed was the blue immensity. He hummed as he watched the clouds transform.

Miles laughed and scrunched up his shoulders as Dr. Peterson stuck the tip of the scope in his ear. Peterson grumbled something incomprehensible under his breath. Miles continued to squirm and giggle until he met the gaze of Francine who was sitting on a chair with her hands folded neatly in her lap. She scowled and shook her head demurely. Miles sat up straight and tried to look serious, but scrunched up his face as Peterson probed his ear. Francine smiled in spite of herself. It had been three weeks since "the incident." They had been to all three of the doctors for whom Miles filed tax returns. None of them could find anything wrong with him. Dr. Ryan had done an MRI and nothing abnormal had shown up. Richards did two CAT scans and another MRI and still nothing. Peterson had been poking, prodding, probing, and pestering Miles for two hours now and he still had not come up with anything but textbook speculations. All three had finally come to the decision that all medical doctors come to when their science fails them, it must be psychological. Francine thanked Dr. Peterson and shook his hand. Miles sprang off the examination table and stood in front of the Doctor and Francine with that smile. Dr. Peterson looked at Francine and she lowered her eyes. He extended his hand for Miles to shake, but Miles seized him in a great, enthusiastic bear hug. Dr. Peterson's arms hung limp at his sides and his face turned bright red. He tried to squeeze out of Miles' grasp, but Miles hugged him harder and snuggled the top of his head against the doctor's face. Francine smiled and shrugged as the doctor looked pleadingly at her. She patted Miles on the back. Miles stopped hugging the doctor. He grabbed the doctor by the shoulders, held him at arm's length, looked at him in the eyes, and, with a beaming smile, said "Gronk." Then he took Francine by the hand and strode out of the office.

Francine sat on the veranda and watched Miles play hide and seek with the kids. She didn't talk on the phone with her sister, or mother and father, she didn't sit and figure out bills or make a grocery list or any of the other thousand things she usually did when she considered herself sitting down and relaxing. She sat and watched Miles play hide and seek with the kids. That is all she did. She watched them the way Miles observed everything, with enthusiastic intent. She could never recall what she was thinking about in those moments or even if she was thinking. Thinking wasn't a concern. She just noticed things she would have never noticed before. It was something of a habit she had picked up from watching Miles. He seemed to notice everything. He would watch a ball of dust roll across the floor, moved by a breeze from under the kitchen door, as if each inch it moved was an event in and of itself. He had once watched a group of aphids crawl up and down the stalk of a flower for three hours, occasionally emitting some weird sound or gesticulating with some strange movement. She sat with him and tried to find out what he saw that was so interesting. She left him to his observation after three minutes. She could find no meaning in the aimless wandering of bugs. It made no sense to just sit there and watch bugs. What was the point? She looked from him to the bugs back to him to see if she could glimpse some clue in the expression of his face to understand what it was he was experiencing, but his expression of intense concentration never changed. The sound of Al Roker's voice distracted her and she left him to watch the bugs so she could go watch Good Morning America. But she began to just watch him watching things. And she noticed things about him she had never noticed, or that might have never been present before, she couldn't determine. There was a comforting silence in just watching. She began to quit trying to figure out what he was thinking, or what it meant for her to watch him watching, and she began to notice things. Or re-notice, she couldn't determine. Everything seemed new and familiar at the same time. She first noticed the way her thoughts, rushing, swirling tried to make sense of the things she watched, to place them in context to something else. After a while she noticed the quiet in her head. Over a period of time, she began to notice the unique shape of bodies, her body in contrast to his body and his body in comparison to the other objects in the room. At night she would watch the children sleeping and notice the shape of their tiny fingers and the difference in the way the two inhaled and exhaled their individual breathes. She noticed intricate differences in textures and smells and sounds and taste. She noticed subtle things about people's personalities, she noticed feelings, she noticed she smiled more.

Sex became important again. No, important wasn't the word; it became sexy and fun and passionate and lusty and tender and naughty and loving again. It became hot. Grand, exciting fucking. They explored each other's bodies as if they had not seen them before.

There were no expectations, no roles, only a creative playfulness, a spontaneous, joyful entanglement, a celebrational dance of flesh.

One early morning, just as the sun began to rise, in the silence and dim light of dawn, Miles stood at the window in their bedroom and looked out. Below him, he saw the children's toys strewn across the backyard. Within the fences of others' backyards, he could see other children's toys, and other people's gardens and swimming pools, and trampolines, and tool sheds, and oak trees and gas grills and lawn mowers. Beyond the fences, houses and driveways, he could see the field, wide, green, and growing with a hundred-different species of wild vegetation. He imagined small creatures awakening from long night sleeps creeping cautiously in search of an early meal, and those returning tired but full and safe from their nocturnal pursuits. He didn't notice that he had started to sway back and forth rhythmically as he stood looking out. The land sloped and rose and flattened and rolled. It spread around, under, and beyond the fences and houses. One landscape intricately, sometimes seamlessly and subtly, sometimes overt and blatant giving way to another. The foothills surfaced above the field. Miles began to make a deep humming noise in his throat. The smooth flow of the hills surrendered to the craggy outcroppings of The Rocky Mountains. A deep pink-orange glow began to spread across the sky. Miles bounced up and down on the balls of his feet. A small bird flew across the sky and perched in a tree in their yard. Miles stopped moving and humming and watched the bird until it flew off again and disappeared into the distance.

Oliphant, of Pinkerton, Oliphant and Monroe called Francine and said there was bad news with Miles' case. The state had declared that Miles' actions, which had forced the police officers to react in the fashion that they had, was a cause for alarm and required that Miles be put on trial to judge his mental stability. It was, in fact, Oliphant said, a legitimate concern, as a citizenship cannot approbate recalcitrant presences effectuating unmitigated heterodoxy, now can we? Francine hung the phone up without saying goodbye. She sat down at the counter and slammed her open hand against the Formica counter top. Then she started to cry.

Miles came from the kitchen holding a bowl full of Crispy Sugar Bombs under his face. He was shoveling the cereal into his mouth as he hummed some made up tune, and milk dripped from the spoon onto his chin and back into the bowl as he ate. That smile beamed across his face when he saw Francine and he sort of skipped toward her. But he saw that she was crying so he placed his bowl on a nearby table and walked slowly toward her. He lifted her head and looked at her with concern. She managed to etch a thin smile across her face when she looked at him. But his touch was so tender and his eyes so sad and worried that she fell into his arms and cried harder. Miles held her tight and the two of them cried together for a long time.

The next week, after work, Miles jumped in his Acura TLX and sped up I-70, past the Pecos exit and on up into the hills to Blackhawk. He knew he was going to make a killing on the roulette wheel.

Paradise Village

I sat on the balcony waiting for Molly to get home. I guess you couldn't call our walkway a balcony, but we had a couple of fold-up chairs that we set up and sometimes sat outside and looked out over the guardrail into the courtyard. I was sitting there hoping that she would just tell me what had happened, well I knew what had happened, but I was hoping she would tell me as opposed to me having to initiate the conversation. But I knew she wouldn't. Our counselor was having us do these exercises in communication, and since she was the one who usually talked about things or brought them up first, she was not supposed to initiate any major conversations. It was up to me, Dr. Forbes had said, to show Molly that I was willing to make an effort to save our marriage. I never really liked that doctor. He was kind of a pompous asshole when I think about it, and I didn't think it was fair to put that kind of pressure on me. It seemed so damn weighty and ominous that I should hold the fate of two beings in my hand, with the decision to talk or not. I know it was important, but he made it seem as if the planet would get flung outta orbit and hurl itself into the sun if I didn't start a conversation. I did talk. I didn't just sit there like an imbecile and stare, and I didn't ignore her. I answered every question she asked, whatever she asked. I just never started the conversation, and this, to them, showed a lack of interest on my part in our relationship. I had never started conversations. I just never knew what to talk about, what was really important, and I didn't want to just talk about anything. I didn't want to look like an idiot. I hate those people who just talk to hear their own voices, who feel they aren't being productive human beings if their mouth isn't moving, who talk about the most asinine things: the price of stamps, how much this quarterback or that pitcher is making, the latest movie star gossip, the way their neighbor dresses or raises their kids, their fucking stock portfolios, how many times they've been to Hawaii, how much they hated their jobs or their wife or husband or lover or mother, that kind of crap. Inane rambling, it sends chills up my fucking spine. I have always been like that. I just don't have much to say about those things. But I always listen and I always answer. So anyway, I had to be the one to ask her why, when both of us knew for God's sake, why there had been a pink stain on a piece of toilet tissue in the bathroom trashcan the previous Friday. It made no sense to me to stir things up when there was nothing we could do about it. It just made things worse, I thought. It is what the fuck it is, was my thinking. Talking about it is like stabbing yourself over and over and over. So I sat in my blue and white nylon foldout chair drinking a beer, and waited for Molly to come home so we could communicate.

On the other side of the apartment complex I saw Marie Gonzalez and her three youngest kids coming up the stairs with several bags of groceries. Any other day I would have helped her, but I didn't feel like it. In fact, I didn't even want to see her or her kids. She saw me and smiled. I held up my beer can and nodded, then went inside my apartment. I lifted a slat on our blinds and peeked out. Marie was a hottie even after having five kids. Sometimes when Xavier, her husband, and Molly weren't around I'd flirt with her and she'd flirt back, but it was never anything serious just a common attraction we liked to acknowledge. She had set the bags of groceries on the ground. She held her eight month old in her right arm and balanced him on her hip. In her right hand she held her purse and searched for her keys with her left hand. The baby was crying and squirming around; I was impressed with her balancing act. Jennifer, her four-year-old was digging through the grocery bags holding up different items. Marie shook her head and Jennifer would slam the item back into the bag. Marie finally found the keys, but they slipped out of her hand as she motioned for Jennifer to grab her two-year-old brother who was crawling too close to the guardrail. I waited to see if the kid was OK, and after Marie smacked him on his little bare leg I closed the slat, got another beer and turned on the tube.

The Gonzalez's had been our neighbors for the entire four years we had lived at Paradise Village; we had seen three of their five kids born. They were eight months, two years old, four, seven, and twelve. Marie worked as a janitor at night and sometimes washed dishes at a Chinese restaurant, and Xavier laid concrete in the summer and did roofing work in the winter. I didn't envy them in that aspect. I couldn't have done it, wouldn't even think about doing it. They'd be worn out by the time they were 55. But, at least they'd have one of those kids to look after them by then. Someone who would be there to pick up groceries, drive them to the doctor when their bones began to soften up and turn to putty, clean up a little, talk to one or the other when one or the other passed away, and so on. I suppose, now, that might have been worth all that labor, not to be alone when you're not needed anymore.

I sat down on the sofa and grabbed the TV remote. I knew nothing was going to be on at 3 o'clock in the afternoon except soap operas, Dr. Phil, and the legion of other talk shows, but I needed something to pass the time. I watched the blurred section over a woman's chest as she exposed herself on Jerry Springer. I briefly thought about going to the computer and jerking off to internet porn, but it felt inappropriate somehow in light of our situation. A Huggies commercial came on. I got up and went into the kitchen to get another beer. I was hungry. I didn't know what time Molly would be home, so I decided to eat a little something before dinner. There was nothing in the fridge except eight beers, a single egg, half-empty condiment jars, a head of wilted leaf lettuce, and a to-go box with a week old piece of lasagna. I knew all the microwave dinners and Chef Boyardee stuff was gone because

I had been surviving on them for the last week. I grabbed a beer and the egg. I opened the cupboard to get a mixing bowl but there were no dishes in there. I opened the dishwasher and it was full of dirty dishes. I wondered how Molly had put up with me for so long. I really was a fuck-up. It was up to me to do the cleaning and shopping during the day since she worked days and I worked nights. But, after the toilet paper thing I had just lost all motivation to do anything. I basically just sat around all day. I had called off of work three times and just sat around the house making to-do lists and drinking beer. I planned to do things. All night I would stay up, lying in bed while Molly slept, thinking about the things that I needed to get accomplished, trying to re-reschedule my life. But, in the morning I only felt more tired and nothing seemed so overly important.

I washed out a bowl and cracked the egg on the side. I was going to scramble it and make a sandwich, we did at least have mayo and a couple pieces of bread, but when it plopped into the bowl there was one of those bloody sacks attached to the yoke. I picked up the bowl and twirled the egg around. The sac swirled around the inside of the bowl. A thin red line clung to the rim and stretched out behind it. "That's all it is," I thought, "just a spot, nothing more." I ran some water and poured the egg into the garbage disposal. It was broken and made a loud, long hollow, sucking sound before it turned on and swallowed the egg down.

I was supposed to have called the manager to get the thing fixed, but I had forgotten. I figured it could wait, and I didn't feel like talking to him and having him send over the chatty maintenance man. It just seemed like too much to deal with. It was enough riding the bus and going to work and having to be around other people. Too many people in a single day was more than I could bear. I felt uncomfortable around people. Incomplete. Like some essential element that made other people "people" was missing in me. And I didn't know how to fit it back in, nor did I really have the will.

I suddenly felt extremely tired, so I went back and sat on the couch. It was 3:15. I was hoping Molly would be home by six. I knew she was going to be pissed off at me because I called off of work. I didn't go to the appointment with her because I had had to work; she had been a bit upset that I didn't try to get the day off or go in late, but she knew we needed the money. So, I knew she was going to be really mad when she found out I didn't go into work or go to the appointment with her. But, I just couldn't do either. The thought of going into work and dealing with my supervisor's "holier-than-thou" attitude and looking into her mousy, big nosed, pale face, and pretending that I was cheery and gave a flying fuck about someone who couldn't connect to the internet caused my stomach to turn. And there was no way I could go and sit in a doctor's office and listen to the sympathetic platitudes of someone I didn't know, and have her try to explain the hows and whys, and why-nots and finally ending with some clichéd explanation that basically meant: sorry, that's life. I flipped through the channels automatically. A set of long legs caught my attention. They were Suzanne Sommer's from a rerun of *Three's Company*. The phone rang. I muted the TV but kept my eye on Sommers as she sashayed across the screen in a one-piece swimming suit. I thought about not answering, but the caller ID showed my brother Leon's number. I like talking to my older brother. He gives me perspective on things and calms me down when I am feeling like I was. He is one of those rare people that actually listens to what a person is saying and doesn't interrupt or give some banal solution he has read from the newest best-selling self-help book, or saw on Dr. Phil. So I picked up the phone.

"Could I 'peak to my new cussin, unca Nate?"

"Elijah?" I asked.

"I 'peak to my cussin, 'kay, unca Nate?"

"Who put you on the phone, baby? Where's your daddy?"

"Mama said I talk to my new cussin."

"E. let me talk..."

"Hello, hello? Nate?" my sister-in-law Silvia said.

"Silvia, what the hell was that?" I said.

"Nate, I'm sorry I thought Molly might be home already from the doctor. What are you doing home? I thought you'd be at work. Are you feeling OK? Elijah and I wanted to surprise her."

"Silvia, where's Leon? Why'd you put that boy on the phone like that? What the fuck, Silvia?"

"I... I wanted to talk to Molly, anyway."

"Silvia, why the hell would you put Elijah on the phone to say some stupid-ass shit like that, huh? Don't you think? What if Molly would have answered and the appointment was bad, huh? What if it turned out like the last two times? What then, Silvia? What the fuck runs through your head, man? Christ!" I yelled and hung up the phone.

I downed the rest of the beer, crushed the can and threw it at the television. I was shaking. I went and got another beer and drank half of it in one swallow. I immediately felt guilty for yelling at her. I wanted to call Silvia back and apologize but the effort seemed too much to deal with. I figured I would call Leon later and have him tell her I was sorry. But at the same time I wanted her to deal with the consequences of her stupidity. She knew what had happened the last two times. What made her think anything would be different this time? Why not wait to find out if everything was cool before making a call like that? I wanted her to think. Just fucking think once outside of her own little Brady Bunch fantasy she tried so hard to create in her life. I wanted her to think about what would have happened if Molly had answered the phone, I wanted her to think about how it felt for Molly to have to see her with Elijah. I wanted her to think about that. I wanted her to know what it felt like. I wanted her to know she was part of a world of stupidity and self-centeredness and I wanted her to feel bad about it and... hurt. I wanted her to apologize to me for being part of a terrible world and not thinking about it or caring. I wanted her to hurt because I did. I pictured her at home crying, not knowing why I had reacted the way I did, and I hated myself for it. She did hurt. She hurt every day just like everybody else and she did her best not to be crushed by it. There was nothing wrong with the idealized life she strived for. That's how she dealt. That's how she kept from being swallowed up by the world. I drank. I wanted to call her back and apologize but I had no clue what to really say. I thought about how bad Molly had felt last time when her mother had called and had done something similar to what Silvia had done. I suddenly wanted to call Molly. I wanted to call her and tell her that I loved her. I wanted to hold her so she could cry on my shoulder, so I could try to suck in all of her inside me, so we could wrap ourselves around each other and just sit somewhere in silence and know we needed each other. I wanted to sit so still with her and just breathe with her. I wanted everything to be the way it had been before. I wanted everything to be different. I finished the rest of the beer. I felt tired, drained, as if I had worked all day doing physical labor.

I went back to the couch and stared at the television. Then the doorbell rang. It was Jennifer Tobin, Marie's four-year-old daughter. I wanted to ignore it but I knew she wouldn't go away. I didn't feel like looking at kids. She rang again, then she knocked, then she rang three more times and knocked at the same time.

"Mr. Nate, Mr. Nate," she yelled, and her sweet, tiny voice made me get up.

I opened the door and she stood there looking up at me with that cherub face and her glowing smile. I could never resist that child. Her curly light, brown hair hung in messy bangs over her forehead and her hazel eyes beamed from above the folds formed by her chubby cheeks. I squatted down eye-level with her. She smelled like peanut butter.

"Young lady, don't you know it's rude not to respect your elder's privacy?' I said.

Her smile wilted.

"Well, what paramount news do you bring me today, angelic one?" I said, holding her face in my hands and tweaking her nose.
She smiled again and giggled. She held up three fingers in front of my face.

"I got four marbles," she said.
I took her hand and held up her index finger.

"That's four, sweetie," I said, and kissed the palm of her hand, "Where are they?"

There was a wet spot on the pocket of her pink corduroy pants; she reached into her pocket and struggled to pull something out. She took out the marbles that she had probably taken out of their goldfish bowl. With her head cocked to one side, she held them in her palm as if she where presenting me the most precious stones on the face of the planet. I held my hands against my cheeks and opened my eyes wide.
"Exquisite," I said, "Where did you get those marvelous things? I've never seen anything like them in the whole world. Beautiful, they are

most definitely beautiful."

She laughed and pushed her hand closer to me.

"Hold 'em," she said, but one of them fell out of her hand, hit the concrete with a sharp clicking sound and rolled off the balcony into the courtyard.

"Uh, oh," she said, and grasped the remaining marbles in her hand. She poked out her bottom lip and her eyes started to tear up. I stood and picked her up.

"Don't worry my little seraph," I said, "We'll go down there and find that gem of yours."

I put her down and moved her bangs from in front of her eyes.

"You wait right here and I'll be right back," I said, and went inside and got another beer. I heard Marie shout something in Spanish and Jennifer answered back in an exasperated tone.

"She's lost her marbles," I said stepping back outside and picking Jennifer up again.

We walked over to the Gonzalez's apartment and Jennifer gave her mother the three remaining marbles.

"She lost one," I said, "I'm just gonna take her downstairs and see if we can find it, OK?"

"Niña malcriada," Marie said, licking her finger and wiping something off of the child's eyebrow. Jennifer laid her head on my shoulder and frowned. "I told you not to bother Mr. Nate."

"Somebody had to do it," I said, "We'll be right back."

"Oh, she's so spoiled. You're spoiled," Marie said.

I smiled and took Jennifer downstairs to find her marble.

I had no idea where the marble would be, and really didn't think we would find it. But, I thought, looking for it would be a good distraction from myself. And like I said, I couldn't resist that little girl; she had me under her thumb. I loved being around her. I loved being around all kids. They astounded me. The energy they have, constant motion, constant changing; their becoming is intoxicating to watch. I wish I still had the wonder and awe they have at discovering the world. I mean, it's true, absolute, unmediated wonder. And in watching their wonder, in watching the awkwardness in which they interact with the world, the clumsy yet determined way they go up a set of stairs, or hold a spoon when they eat, watching this makes me think about how much time I'm wasting being... unhappy. I marvel at those tiny replicas of us and how much potential they have. God, it's sad that they become us. But, Jennifer was something special to me. She burned her presence into me. Wholly.

Molly and I were eating dinner with the Gonzalez's one night when Jennifer was about six months old. I was holding her and she was tugging at my nose, my ears, and moustache. She was the absolute cutest thing I'd ever seen. I held her against my chest and kissed the top of her head. I felt something surge through me like a mild electric shock through my entire body. I felt... light for a moment, just sort of weightless. I just held her close to me for a moment until it subsided. And even now, eight years later, after the divorce, after rehab, after moving out of the country to teach Chinese children English then returning back to Colorado, at times when I am most happy or sad I can still feel the presence of that little girl on my chest.

I set her down when we got to the courtyard. She grabbed my hand and we walked to where she thought the marble might be. The smell of smoke drifted through the air with flakes of blackened paper. Two boys, about eleven or twelve were lighting old newspapers on fire in one of the old dilapidated barbeque grills. The taller of the two wore a black t-shirt with the word "mistake" printed in white lettering that was supposed to appear as if it was melting off the shirt. The short boy wore a hooded gray sweater with Nirvana printed on the front. Jenny sneezed and I flailed the air with my hands to get the smoke and ash away from her. I glared at the boys. They stared back and threw more paper into the flames. Jenny let go and ran to the old pop machine.

"I want one," she said, pushing the button where a water-stained and faded label for grape Fanta was. The lock on the machine had been jimmied open and hung from the door by a single rusted bolt. The door bounced open and shut as Jenny pushed the Fanta button. I set my beer on top of the machine. I looked inside the machine but it was empty. There were no can racks, no mechanisms, no lights or wires. There was nothing but dust and a few dead leaves inside.

"It's broken baby," I said. "Maybe we can get one later, OK?" She looked at me as if she didn't believe me, but I guess she figured it wasn't that important because she didn't harp on the subject like she usually did.

"I have some pudding," she said, and walked on.

She stopped in front of the sliding glass door to the weight room and pressed her face against the glass. There was a single barbell with an uneven number of 20 pound weights, the old cement ones encased in plastic, a bench press with one of the arms missing, a drinking fountain that didn't work and was encrusted with a greenish-white calcium built around the knob, and dried up spit lines down the front of it. A used condom was thrown in front of the bathroom door. I could smell mildew. I pulled Jenny away from the glass.

"Don't lean on the glass, honey. It's dirty," I said, wiping a spot of dust from her forehead.

"My marble," she said, and pulled away from me, running toward something on the ground. She picked up a small oval stone and held it up to me.

"That's kinda like it. But, remember it was more round, shiny, and made of glass, remember?"

She nodded her head up and down so hard I thought she might hurt her neck. Her bangs bounced over her forehead and she smiled. She held the rock in her hand for a moment and studied it, then dropped it and walked on.

The second she reached for the shiny object I saw it, but she grabbed it before I could reach her and the piece of glass sunk into the palm of her hand. She hollered. It was a shrill, piercing scream that sent a shiver through my body like a current of icy needles. Yet, my body grew heavy; my arms and legs turned to iron and it felt like days before I reached her and swooped her up. It wasn't a big piece of glass, but she was opening and closing her fist pushing the shard further into her palm. I tried to calm her down and comfort her, but her screams got louder. She grabbed me around my neck and I could feel the wet stickiness of her blood smear across it. She flailed. Her hand slapped across my right cheek. I set her down so I could get a better look at her hand. She clung to me around my legs. When I finally pried her from my legs to investigate her hand, the two boys from the grill had migrated over to us and stood staring.

"What'd ya do to her, dude?" Nirvana said.

"Shut the fuck up kid and get me something to clean her up with," I said.

He stared down at me, expressionless. His friend pushed him and he ran to the weight room. Jenny howled. I managed to open her hand and saw the glass embedded in her palm. An unusual amount of blood was pouring from the wound. I was stunned that so much could be coming out of something small. I tried to pull the glass out, but she kept pulling away from me, hollering louder every time I touched her hand.

"¿Qué pasa?, ¿Qué pasa?" I heard Marie yelling as she ran down the stairs. "What's wrong? Xavier, ¿qué le pasa a Jenny?"

I turned around and saw Xavier walking through the courtyard gate. He looked up at Marie and she pointed to me. "Mi bebé, Xavier what's wrong with her, hurry," she yelled. Xavier ran to us. When Jenny saw her father she screamed louder and ran to him. He picked her up and looked at me.

"She grabbed a piece of glass, man," I said, and tried to show him, but Jenny pulled away. Xavier glared at me. Jenny grabbed his hair, and I saw a streak of maroon dull his glossy, black hair. He said something to her in Spanish and trotted to the stairs where Marie was waiting.

"God, man, I'm so sorry. We just gotta get the glass and she'll be alright," I said, following behind them.

"It's OK, it's OK" Xavier said, walking faster and waving me to stay put. "I'll get it out, I'll get it out."

I stopped. I watched them walk back up the stairs. Marie took Jenny and held her tight against her. They looked back at me, turned around and walked up to their apartment, and shut the door.

"You still need this, man," the kid said, and handed me some paper towels.

"Damn, dude, he's got blood all over him," Nirvana said to his friend as they strolled back to the grill.

I wiped the blood from my neck, face, and hands. A little brown stain remained in the lines of my hands. I went to the weight room bathroom and washed up. I went back outside, grabbed my beer from the top of the pop machine. It was warm, but I downed it. I was still shaky; I felt light-headed and thought I was going to vomit. I squatted down and leaned against the wall. I watched Jenny's blood soak into the concrete and start to dry. It would probably be there until the apartment complex was finally condemned and torn down. I closed my eyes and saw Jenny's wide, shocked and terrified little hazel eyes in my head. I opened my eyes. I tried to hold it back, but I felt my eyes tearing up. I covered my face and it all fell out of me like a heavy rain. I sobbed. I sobbed so hard the muscles in my neck, shoulders, and belly ached. I couldn't control it. It was as if something tangible, thick, gooey, and wet was trying to secrete itself out of my body. I thought about Jenny's hand and I sobbed harder; I thought about Marie and Xavier's faces when they looked at me and about the audacity and right they had to look at me like that. I thought about Silvia and what I had said to her, I thought about her weeping in front of my nephew and his confusion and fear. I thought about my brother. I thought about Molly and the pink tissue in the trashcan, and I sobbed harder. I thought about the fact that Dr. Forbes was in our lives, I thought about my job, all the good and bad things that I had done and would do. I looked at the two boys. They were laughing at me, and through my sobs I laughed with them. But, I sobbed for them too and their families, and I laughed and sobbed because I knew what a pathetic sight I made, and because I didn't care. I stood up and faltered between convulsing sobs and hysterical laughing. I wiped my eyes, but the tears kept coming. I was gasping to catch my breath and my body heaved with coughing. I tried to walk but I staggered and had to hold myself up on the pop machine. I looked at the two boys again. They were still laughing, wiping their eyes pretending they were crying. I flipped them off. They flipped me back off and started laughing. I started toward them, but I saw Molly's car pull into the apartment complex parking lot. I didn't want her to see me crying so I jumped the gate around the back of the complex and started walking.

I walked to City Park. I sat on the hill behind the Museum of Natural History and looked at the city skyline. A deep purple infused with orange in the sky over the mountains. It calmed me with its vastness. I felt a bit more relaxed. I felt exhausted. I lay back in the grass and shut my eyes. I thought about leaving; I thought that it would be best for everybody involved with me if I just left. For a couple of hours I lay there and contemplated how and why I should leave. The fact was that I would have missed Molly too much. It was simple as that. This realization calmed me down and I decided to go home and talk to Molly. I decided to go home, hold her and listen to what she had to say, to discuss with her what we could do to be closer. What I needed to do to make her feel happy. I decided to try to make her life wonderful. I felt a new energy. My head was clear and felt confident. I got up and headed home to my wife.

I saw the Monroe Tavern as I was crossing Colfax and decided to have a beer before I went home. A few friends of mine were there and we started playing darts. Then we started making bets on throws for shots. Then we started buying each other beers and waxing nostalgic about the drunken drama we had involved ourselves in over the years. It was 10:15pm when I looked at the clock. I tried to leave, but my friend Norman bought another round. So of course I had to buy one too. Then someone else bought another round and so on and so on. It was quarter to one when I finally staggered out the door. I went up the street to Singapore Café and ordered a box of shrimp fried rice.

I tripped going through the gate to the courtyard. The two boys were gone, but it looked like they had finished tearing the grill off its pole because it lay upside down next to the pole. They had written fuck in big letters from the ashes on the concrete picnic table. I saw the pop machine. I kissed the tips of my fingers on my right hand and held them out toward the machine. "I'm so sorry, little angel," I mumbled, and went upstairs. I stopped in front of the Gonzalez's door. The lights were out, but I tried to listen to hear if anyone was still awake. I banged my head on the door as I tried to put my ear against it. I staggered away on tiptoes

I started to get the spins a little, and I had to try three times before I got the key in the door of our apartment. The kitchen light was the only light on. Molly's coat was thrown over the back of the couch. There were a couple pieces of paper sticking out of the pocket.

I took them out and read them. They were prescriptions. One was for Vicodin; the other was for some type of antibiotic. I pushed them back into her pocket. I looked in the bedroom. Molly was curled up on top of the bed, her clothes and shoes still on. There were two beer cans on the nightstand next to the alarm clock.

"Moll, you up?" I whispered, "You OK?"

She didn't answer. I started to go in and sit on the bed and wake her up, but I didn't. I stood there and looked at her for a long moment, then I remembered my fried rice. I went into the kitchen, grabbed a fork from the dishwasher, wiped it on my shirt and ate fried rice over the sink.

Failure of the Sun

Eliot Turner sat in his recliner sipping on Maker's Mark and watching several moths crawl around the inside of his fireplace. The house was dark except for the dim orange glow of a small halogen lamp that sat on the bar behind him. He stared at the moths as they crawled over the floor and wall of the fireplace, every once in a while, one or two would spring into a dizzying, erratic aerial spiral, then land randomly in another spot. He took a sip of whiskey and set the glass on the table, a melting piece of ice slipped from its position on the top and dinged against the side of the glass. Eliot took a cigarette out of his pack and lit it. He inhaled the smoke deeply and let it out in a dense stream from his mouth and nose. Then he tossed the lit match in the fireplace. "Are they really attracted to flame?" he thought. None of the creatures approached the dying flame. He lit another match and tossed it. This one caught the left wing of one of the insects as it fluttered off the wall. It spiraled to the floor and crawled aimlessly in confusion. It tried to fly again but it could only lift the wing that had not been burnt. It flew spastically around and around in a tight circle. After a moment it stopped and just crawled along the edge of the hearth. It crawled and clung to the outer hearth and tried again to fly. It fell onto the carpet and tried again. It started to spin around again but the tiny hairs on its legs became entangled in the fabric of the carpet. The creature did this several more times, but it could not free itself from the carpet. Eliot watched as the moth struggled to fly. He remembered having read something years ago about what moths meant in some Eastern religions. Because of their irresistible attraction to and the destruction by the light of a flame, they were equated with the soul's mystic, selfless, self-sacrificing love of the divine. The surrendering of the ego-self to the will of the divine grace. In some dream interpretations they are seen as symbols of personal weakness or deception. The animal, flapping its damaged wings at a furious rate, continued to try to free itself. For a moment Eliot thought of freeing the creature, but he didn't.

"What brought the kindred spider to that height,
Then steered the white moth thither in the night?
What but design of darkness to appall?
If design govern in a thing so small," he said and saluted the moth with his glass.

They were common Miller moths, a whole huge plague of them had descended upon Denver, and they were everywhere. Eliot had startled them inside of his kitchen cupboards, his dryer, his sock drawer, light fixtures, the tops of paintings, the pockets on his pool table, the bottoms of the furnace, they flew out from under the refrigerator carrying little balls of dust with them; the air conditioner blew out at least six or seven every time he turned it on, and a few had even found refuge under the rim of his toilet. They flew out of the vents in his car, from under the lawn mower, from the ceiling of his shed, from out of the poorly folded tops of boxes of forgotten things, from the crevices of concrete that had cracked on his patio, from his attic, from his basement. He had even begun to dream about them. There was no place in the city inaccessible to the moths. He had read in the pull-out section of the newspaper the day before yesterday an article written by a local entomologist. The article stated that conditions produced from the exceptionally wet winter months were extremely favorable for the moth's reproduction and they produced in the range of tens to a hundreds of millions of offspring. They migrated to the mountains to feed on the nectar of the flowers and mate, then flew back down to the plains to lay their eggs for the following spring, then die. Eliot took another puff on his cigarette and blew the smoke into the fireplace. A few moths dislodged from the wall and flew drunkenly into one another then settled back down.

Eliot drained his glass, stood up and walked over to the bar to pour himself another drink. He looked up at the clock behind the bar. Claire was going to be there in forty minutes, and he was nervous. He had not seen or even thought about her in years, but now, since he had seen her last week at the mall she was all he thought about. It seemed a bit too coincidental that he should see her almost exactly ten years to the day after the breakdown. He wondered if she may have planned it as some part of one of her schemes, but he immediately dismissed the thought. Those types of thoughts were pre-successful Eliot, paranoid, self-important ideas that led to a dark place in his psyche. He was beyond all that messy doubt and confusion. He had had his time in hell and come out for the better. He refused to go back. He walked up the three stairs leading to his front door and turned on the light switch. The chandelier, a French model with alabaster sconces, lit the room. Nine or ten moths flew out from among the crystals. Eliot looked out over his living and dining room. He smiled to himself. He lived a good life, he thought. He was a writer, even though it was only "mainstream fiction" books he wrote. It was a job that allowed him the independence that most of the slaves that were his neighbors, who hated their menial existence, envied. He was a celebrity in this suburban sanctuary. He was rich and had the biggest house on the block, a six-bedroom, three-bathroom house with a finished basement and furnished in nothing but Drexel Heritage, Ethan Allen, and Thomasville furniture. It made him feel good that a lot of his neighbors hated the fact that a black man had more than they did. And he sported his wealth. He drove a Mercedes S Class Maybach and had a mint condition 1969 Corvette Stingray he kept in his garage to show off when he had parties. He wore clothes from Homer Reed and Abercrombie and Fitch, and threw lavish parties for the holidays and made up special occasions, usually when he had purchased some new piece of furniture or art or published another book. He had surprised himself with how easily he had become comfortable with being a socialite. He looked around and smiled again, but the usual pride that he felt was gone. There was apprehension, and he knew it was because of Claire.

He had made this life for himself in just six years. He had moved out to the suburbs to isolate himself. At the age of thirty-five he started writing action/adventure novels and left the idea of Claire and a "serious literary" career behind him. After the failure of his first and last "literary" novel, the split-up with Claire, the breakdown, and the hospital, he had disappeared and lived in the basement of his uncle Ray's house, a man who had decided to quit talking fifteen years prior and had never said a word since. No one in his family knew why Ray had quit talking. He had shown up to Christmas dinner one year and at the end of the night, out of the clear blue, he announced, "Because things is how things is, there really ain't nothing else to say about 'em. So I won't be saying nothing else about anything no more." And he didn't. No one knew or ever found out what the "things" were he was referring to. He never uttered another word. There was speculation and anger that he was referring to his relationship with the other members of the family, but those ideas were put to rest as he attended and was friendly and happy at every family get together. It was eventually just accepted that Ray didn't want to talk and that was that. Eliot stayed with Ray for four years, and it was Ray's calm silence that helped Eliot more than any of the therapy or medication he took. Nothing bothered Ray. He loved to garden and watch TV, and that's all he really did. But if it rained or hailed and destroyed his garden, he'd just buy new plants. If the power went out and he couldn't watch television, he'd sit on his porch and watch the people walking by in the neighborhood or stare up at the stars at night. Living with Ray was the most peaceful time in Eliot's life. The calm brought inspiration and Eliot decided to write again. He intended to write a "serious literary" novel about Claire and himself, but it turned into a novel about a paranormal private detective that stopped The Rapture, and he found that story much more fun to write.

Ray's Zen-like attitude was extremely helpful, and so were the

Xanax, in their own intensely stupefying way, but writing was the most effective method of quieting The Noise. The Noise had been the source of his breakdown, and was still the center of his fear. He wasn't certain when he became aware of The Noise, but he remembered it had started like a soft electro-static hiss in the background of his life, a doubting uncertainty that tinted all his thoughts. And actually, when he had reflected upon it in his therapy sessions, he realized The Noise had always been there. He could not remember a time when it had not been. Eventually, as his life seemed to unravel, the hiss increased in duration and volume. It became like the sound of the constant burning of a small fire, the crackling of burning branches. It was the accompaniment to the bombardment of ceaseless thoughts of being trapped. He felt trapped by his job, by the position in life it afforded him, by his inability to articulate himself artistically, by the lack of vision to see opportunities to propel himself forward and be successful, by being a nobody. But he held onto the fact that at least he had Claire. But he didn't for long, and when she left him because he "had turned so negative" the crackling of the fire turned into a roar of flood waters. And then when his first novel, the one thing that he had seen as his way out, his pedestal above mediocrity, above the herd, above the system, the thing that had been his very identity, had failed terribly with readers and critics, he dissolved, and the roar of waves exploded into an assault of deafening, incapacitating white noise. The terror of things unraveling, the idea of having no control over the decisions in his life and the uncertainty of that fact literally floored him. He had moments of sheer terror in which his heart raced, he could not breath and he fainted. His parents hospitalized him, and he stayed in the Swedish Medical Center's psych ward for eight months. After he was released, it was thought it would be best if he moved somewhere calm, so he moved in with Ray.

But he changed all that. The book was published by Knopf Doubleday and it sold well. He made some money off of it and it landed at number 74 on Barnes & Noble's bestseller list. He decided that "mainstream" was the way to go. He had worked hard to insulate himself against anything that might cause his new, compact, ordered life to unfurl. He moved out to the suburbs to get away from the city and the "writerly life-style" he had imagined he would live in the city. He quit hanging out with other writers, especially his old "literary" writing group. Their supercilious egos oozed a particularly vile and ferocious insincerity. Their pseudo-intellectual prattle weighted with the competition to be more ironic and clever than each other had worn skin piercingly thin with Eliot. When he had solidified his success with his second novel, the condescending remarks he had received from his friends concerning the success of his first book, "good idea to write a formula book to get your foot in the door," turned to jabs about "selling-out." So Eliot left the little circle of MFAers struggling with their literary art and moved to the one place he knew they would never want to associate themselves with anyway. Fuck it, yes he had snubbed a bunch of want-to-be-intellectual-hacks and he had succeeded. He was proud of it. The failure of that life was now very far behind him. He had succeeded and it had really been all he ever wanted. He had realized the dream, gotten his piece of the pie and he was not at all ashamed or guilty about it. People wanted stories and he wrote them. He was as happy as a hipster at a coffee shop; he was comfortable and satisfied with his life.

But now Claire, who had been a part of that old life, was back. And the anxiety that he had thought he had mastered was back. But he pushed it away. That was the thinking of the old Eliot. The new Eliot, the successful Eliot, was going to view Claire's reappearance as a good thing. Finally, he would have the woman he wanted to go with the success he earned. He still loved her, and he hoped, no, he knew, she still loved him.

He had been playing the role of an old pioneer storyteller at one of the neighborhood kids' birthday party. Marilyn Foster, the mother of little Benjamin Jr. and Eliot's recent affair, had asked him to do it, and her husband Ben had thought it was a swell idea. Eliot did it because he liked the power of the secret he had. It was immensely satisfying being at a family event with the wife he was fucking and the man who was completely unaware of that fact. He reveled in the idea that he had made Ben and three other of his neighbors cuckolds, and then sat down at the same dinner table and discussed the stock market or baseball with them. At one gathering he had sat with all four of them at once and ate their steaks and drank their wine. Ben Jr.'s party was held at Big Fun amusement palace in the local mall. Eliot had rented a buckskin suit and a raccoon skin hat from a costume store. He had sat for two hours making up frontier stories for loud, spoiled, runny-nosed white kids and he had started to need a drink about a half an hour into it. When the party was over he shook Ben's hand, clandestinely squeezed Marilyn's ass, rushed out of the fun palace without taking off his costume and headed for the bar in the Red Robin restaurant on the second level of the mall. As he rode the escalator he heard a woman's soft and sultry voice say, "My, how postmodern, a black Daniel Boone." Within the two seconds it took him to respond there was an eternity of confusion in which he was bombarded by a wave of emotion. He had recognized the voice physically before it registered in his mind; a warm shiver shot up his spine and throughout his body making his stomach and scrotum tighten. He felt a quick wave of dizziness pass over him like a blast of cold air. Then his mind grasped who it was and the short circuiting of the fight-or-flight response kicked into overdrive. He felt fear, but yearning as well, anger and relief, sadness and joy. He felt an increasing pressure on his temples, and had the urge to not turn around and run up the escalator without looking back. But there was also pride. He turned and Claire smiled at him. A soft, distant hiss sounded in his ears.

"Hey," he said.

"Hey yourself," she said, and flipped her hair back over her right shoulder.

Eliot stared at her. She was still the most stunningly beautiful woman he had ever seen. She was half Somalian and half Mexican, the daughter of a cocktail waitress and an American navy man. Her hair, with a black sheen that made it look as if it shimmered, flowed over her shoulders down past the small of her back. She wore a white, strapless, form fitting sun-dress. She looked like some ancient island princess, some Indian goddess from a Hindu relief in a temple. To Eliot she was woman incarnate.

Claire joined Eliot in the Red Robin bar and drank a Cape Cod while he sat nervously in his Daniel Boone clothes and downed three glasses of Jack Daniels black label. They made small talk. Eliot told her about his writing success (it was obligatory), and she told him she had read two of his books and liked them. She told him she had been a design consultant for the last four years. They talked about movies they had seen, other books they had read, the economy, and other banal but safe topics. She finished her drink and scooted the glass away from herself. Eliot knew she was about to leave and he didn't want her to go. He was hooked, again. He wanted, achingly, to hold her face in his hands and feel her mouth on his. He asked her if she wanted to go have dinner, but she said she had a prior engagement. He felt a deep visceral disappointment, as if she had kicked him in the stomach. But she placed her hand on his cheek and told him it was great to see him and gave him one of her cards and told him to call her. He called her ten minutes later and they planned a date for the following week.

Eliot downed his drink, poured himself another, and turned on Pandora Radio. The voice of Al Green floated into the room. Eliot began to sway to the music. He poured himself another drink, got his cigarettes, lit one, and started slow dancing with an imaginary partner. He swayed his invisible partner slowly back and forth across the hardwood floor. "You smell incredible, is that Shalini?" he whispered into her invisible ear, then kissed her invisible cheek. "I've missed you. It's been too long," he said and gently moved a displaced curl from her forehead with his finger. "Yes, sweetheart I know, and I love you too," he said, then swung her around and dipped her just in time for the end of the song. He bowed to his partner, finished his drink then leaned into her. "What?" he said, "You want to fuck the shit out of me, why of course that's OK my dear, right here on the dance floor? Yes, that would be fine," he said, then burst into laughter almost tripping as he walked up the stairs back to the bar. The doorbell rang and he stumbled rushing to the door. It was Claire.

Eliot stared at her and she smiled. She was dressed in a fire red evening gown. He continued staring and she raised her eyebrows.

"Can I come in, Mister?" she said.

"Yeah... yeah come on. I'm sorry. You just look... stunning, amazingly so."

"Thank you, you look nice too. You didn't say you want to go dancing."

"Say what?"

"Dancing. I'm not going dancing with you tonight because you still don't know how to dance, Eliot," she said smiling. Eliot looked at her confused.

"You should close your window before you start dancing with your imaginary friends. Your neighbors might get the wrong idea."

"You saw that?"

"Every step."

Eliot covered his eyes with his hand and shook his head. "Oh shit. I am so embarrassed. And you just stood there watching?"

"Sí, señor."

He shook his head and smiled at her.

"Was there not one good move?"

Claire shook her head.

"No matter. But no, dancing isn't what I had planned. I thought we could have some dinner and go to a show after that. How does that sound?

"Well it depends on your choices, sir."

"We'll go see *The Lion King*; I managed to get some seats up close. Then we'll get some mussels. You still like mussels, right? That sound OK to you, Madame?"

"OK, as long as there's no dancing."

"No dancing."

After the performance, at Marlowe's, they sat at a table by a window. The dim flicker of a candle on the table cast a yellowish glow upon their faces. A moth violently thumped against the window determined to get to the small swarm of his brethren that crawled across the window on the other side and flew around pestering people that walked by on the street. The low murmur of voices from the other customers mixed with the soft sound of a piano being played from across the room. It was a busy night. Waiters and waitresses dressed in white shirts with bow ties and black slacks rushed to and from tables with plate laden trays. Eliot had requested his regular table out of the way of the traffic. Claire sat silently sipping a glass of merlot, and Eliot waved over their waiter to bring him another Jack on the rocks.

They talked about the complexity of the staging for the show and marveled at what a herculean task of scheduling and labor it must be to transport the show across the country. Eliot joked about the fat man that sat next to Claire who was obviously too big for his chair and kept trying to adjust himself to get comfortable. Eliot said he was just trying to cop a feel of Claire's leg. Claire said he smelled like breakfast sausage. They both laughed, then felt guilty for laughing at the man, but laughed again as Eliot mimicked the way the man wiggled in his seat.

"Stop, Eliot. We're terrible," Claire said trying to catch her breath.

"I know, right. I'm sorry. It's not him personally. I'm sure he's a great person. It's just the situation is funny as hell. Something straight from an old Chaplin flick."

"You'll need to put him in a story."

"Yeah, I'll make him a villain. The Thunderous Dr. Wiggles whose shaking girth causes seismic disturbances across the city."

"No, seriously. He seems like a great character. What causes a man to get that big? Why was he at that particular show alone? Is he married? Is he divorced? Is he rich, poor? How did he feel having to wiggle into that seat?"

"I'll have him smash his way through New York and Wall Street and instead of the military using conventional weapons to stop him, they'll pile a giant mountain of pork products at the end of Broadway and he'll be destroyed by heart failure from overeating, best-seller material," he said laughing.

Claire did not laugh. She turned and looked out the window. The moth was still trying to get outside.

Eliot heard the soft hiss of static echo in his ears.

"Oh you know I'm just joking, girl. I'm not like that. You know me, Mr. bleeding-heart."

The smile returned. "Oh geez, yes. Please don't remind me of those days. You and Tyrone and your ethical tirades, fun but very annoying after the first few hours."

Eliot laughed. The static dissipated. He told her about the new book he was writing.

Claire listened, genuinely listened. It was one of her most endearing qualities, one of the things that had irresistibly drawn him to her and kept him enamored. When he finished talking she asked him questions. Some of the questions he answered, some he told her she would have to wait and read about.

There was a lull in the conversation. It was uncharacteristically uncomfortable. He felt as if he had talked too long. But Claire looked at him for a long moment and then smiled.

Do you want another glass of wine?" Eliot asked

"Sure. So when are you going to start writing serious again?"

The static distorted her words and they sounded fuzzy and thin, as if spoken from far away.

"What?"

"Do you think you'll ever try to write another serious book again?

"What I write is serious, what do you mean?"

"Don't get defensive, I mean literary. You know exactly what I mean. Something like your very first novel? I loved that book. I've read it twice actually."

Eliot searched in his pocket for his cigarettes and lighter. Then he remembered he couldn't smoke in the restaurant. The waiter brought him another drink and asked Claire if she wanted another glass of wine, she nodded. The incessant thumping of the moth against the glass fused with the static. He needed a cigarette.

"I'm going to go out for a smoke. I'll be right back OK?"

Claire, resting her chin on her folded hands, looked at him and smiled.

"I'm sorry, I didn't mean to bring up a sore subject. I was just wondering," she said.

"No, it's OK. Really. I just... I mean I have fun writing the books that I write. I make a good living writing those stories. Plus, I don't miss all that pompous... bullshit that goes along with all that 'serious fiction'. I just tell stories now."

"It doesn't have to be pompous, Eliot. But anyway, I wasn't saying anything bad about what you're doing, I was just wondering if you had thought about writing something else. You're a wonderful writer; everything you write is good. I was just making conversation, OK?"

"No, no really it's fine, I didn't mean to make a big deal about it. But no, to answer your question I haven't thought about writing anything else. I'm pretty satisfied with this thing right now. And Claire, I appreciate the compliment, but nobody liked that book."

Claire shook her head and smiled.

"I do."

Eliot nodded and turned to go out and smoke. The hiss receded again.

They were silent during the drive back to Eliot's house. Eliot smoked and hung his cigarette arm out the window so the smoke wouldn't bother Claire any more than it did. A Santana song played on the radio. Claire leaned back in her seat, eyes closed, moving her head to the music. When the song was over she turned the radio down.

"So you really like Marlowe's, huh?"

"Yeah, it's alright I guess, why?"

"Well, you have a regular seat, you know the staff by name, they know what you drink. You must go there a lot."

Eliot flicked his cigarette out the window, looked over at her and shrugged. "They have good food."

"Hmm. You take anybody else there regularly?"

Eliot exhaled a soft laugh. "What is this?" he said looking in his rearview mirror. "Are you prying?"

"As a matter of fact I am. I don't want to be one of your little hoochies that you take to your regular bar to show off," she said and raised her eyebrows.

Eliot laughed again. "Don't worry, that's my personal get-away-from-it-all spot. No one goes there but me." he lied, "What are you jealous or something?"

"Don't get crazy, Eliot. You know what I'm talking about."

He turned to her again and winked at her. "God, you're so... very beautiful," he said.

She turned and looked out the window with a big smile spread across her face.

As they turned into his parking lot he saw the light on in Foster's living room and the shadow of a figure behind the curtains. When Eliot turned the car off, the light went off in the house. Eliot smiled to himself. He got out of the car and walked around to the other side to let Claire out. He locked the car door with his remote and tripped as he was walking up the steps to his door. Claire steadied him and they went into the house and closed the door.

Elliot woke from a familiar dream in which he could never remember any of the details. All he ever experienced when he woke up was a feeling of relief. The type of feeling that one has when they realize they have escaped from a situation that could have ended with dire consequences. That anxious, exhausting, exhilaration of having just dodged a bullet. He lay still with his eyes closed and his night thoughts disintegrating as consciousness slowly returned to him. The airy spaciousness of dream faded into light-headed dizziness. He yawned, felt the pasty thickness that coated his mouth and tasted his foul breath. He smacked his lips, frowned and adjusted his pillow beneath his head. Then the pain of the headache shot through his body and he felt the familiar nausea. He turned over to get up. The dizziness increased. He reached behind himself to push himself up and touched something. He turned and saw Claire still sleeping next to him. Through the dull throbbing of his head the hazy memories of the night before returned to him. He managed a smile.

He propped himself up on his elbow and leaned down to kiss her on the cheek. A stark pain exploded in his skull. He fell back onto his pillow rubbing his temples; he felt dizzy and his stomach churned. He waited until the room stopped bucking and shifting and the pain subsided to a dull throb before he got up, groping his stomach, and staggered into the bathroom. He relieved himself, swabbed a toothbrush through his mouth, and grabbed three Alka-Seltzers from a thin glass jar then shuffled into the kitchen. He poured himself a glass of Red Bull, dropped the three tablets into the glass, watched the beige foam slide over the rim, then drank it down. He sat down in his recliner to let the medicine take effect. The moth from the night before, still entangled in the carpet, lay dead at the foot of the hearth. As he smoked the day's first cigarette, Eliot tried to move the moth out of his sight by blowing smoke at it. He didn't want to look at the dead creature, but the effort to bend over and pick the thing up seemed too much for his pounding head. He tried to stretch out and move the thing with his foot, but it was just out of reach. Eliot shrugged, reclined the chair and closed his eyes.

Claire did not wake up as he fell back into the bed. He lay motionless for a moment then turned onto to his right side and braced himself with his elbow. He followed the smooth contours of her body underneath the paisley sheet with just his eyes. They came to rest on her face and he traced the shape of her lips, her cheekbone, the side of her small round nose, the slant of her eyes, the thin line of her eyebrow, and her eyelashes with the tip of his finger. A soft moan escaped with her breath, and Eliot leaned down and brushed his lips against hers. He continued to stare at her, his eyes transfixed on her face and a thin crooked smile etched across his face. She turned onto her back with a groan and rested her right arm over her forehead.

"I hate you, Eliot Turner," she said through a half smile. "I haven't been hung over in years. You're a terrible influence."

Eliot kissed her deep and full upon her lips. She wrapped her arms around his neck. They pulled apart reluctantly and Eliot sat up and grabbed a glass of water and three aspirin from his night stand and handed them to her. She sat up, took the aspirin, and downed them with the water.

"Thank you," she said. She looked at him and saw that he was dressed. "How long have you been up?"

"Long enough to get you this," he said reaching back to the nightstand then handing her a large Starbucks cup. "Venti, White Chocolate Mocha with a double shot of espresso and soy. That's right, right? You still drink these?"

"Oh thank you, thank you, thank you. You remembered. You are my knight with shining Starbucks, the god of coffee."

She took the cup, closed her eyes and took a long slow sip. When she finished she stared at Eliot over the rim of the cup and smiled.

"Oh my God, this is so good. I so needed this. You, my love, are what is right about the world."

My love. The words reverberated in Eliot's mind like the calm vibrations of a rin gong. The bluesy doubt and mild depression from the hangover dissolved. He felt confident and complete. His mother used to say that 'the sun was shining on you' when life seemed to hand one a gift. The sun had truly shined upon his life, he thought. He stared at her and the look he gave her made her body tingle. She placed the cup on the other nightstand and laid back. Eliot leaned over her and kissed her hard, passionately. He kissed her down her neck, over her breast and stomach until he lodged his face between her legs. Claire arched her back and sighed. The doorbell rang. They tried to ignore it but it rang three more times in rapid succession. Eliot lifted his head and rested it on Claire's stomach. The bell rang again.

"Fucking shit," Eliot mumbled and got up.

Claire wrapped herself up in the sheet, grabbed her coffee and leaned back against the headboard.

"This should be fun," she said.

The doorbell rang twice again before Eliot got to the door.

"Christ Almighty, I'm here, what, who is it?" he said, as he approached the door. He accidently kicked a slipper that he had left out. A group of moths flew out from inside the slipper. He batted one and it fell to the ground dazed. He swung the door open with a jerk and a frown on his face. "What," he growled.

It was a bright, sunny morning and Marilyn Foster stood shiny and smiling at the door. She was dressed in a pair of yoga pants and a sports halter top. She had her hair tied back in a ponytail. A thin sheen of sweat shown on her chest. She looked down at her fitness watch to check either the time or her pulse.

"Hi. Did I wake you? The boys went fishing and I just finished a jog, so I thought I would stop in and see how you're doing?" she said, stepping past him into the house.

Eliot stood in the door and watched as she prowled his living room with her eyes. She said something else but he didn't hear her. He was deafened by the static in his head. He felt light-headed and leaned against the door.

"Doesn't that sound fun," she said, standing in front of him with her hands on her hips.

Through the static he heard the top stair of the staircase creak. He closed the front door, and leaned against it.

"What?" he said.

"Wine and cheese in Estes Park," she said it slowly as if spelling it out. "Ben will be out of town on that weekend and we…"

"Mmm, that sounds good," Claire said coming down the stairs wrapped in the bed sheets.

Eliot's shoulders and head slumped.

"Good morning, I'm Claire. It's nice to meet you," she said letting the sheet slip off her left shoulder as she reached her hand out to shake Marilyn's.

Marilyn stared at Claire with wide, unbelieving eyes as if Claire was some holy or unholy apparition. Her hand rose automatically and she placed it inside Claire's.

"So you were saying something about a wine and cheese tasting in Estes. You think we could make it, baby?" Claire said, turning to Eliot.

"Mmm," Eliot mumbled.

Marilyn's face turned a shiny maroon. She pulled her hand away from Claire's as if the latter had pinched her.

"Oh God, I'm sorry. I'm so sorry. I didn't know he, I didn't know you had company. I just… I was jogging and I… I just stopped by," she said rushing past Claire toward the door. Eliot opened the door and Marilyn nearly ran out. Eliot closed the door and he and Claire stared at one another. In the next moment the silence was interrupted with the dull thud of the Foster's front door being slammed shut.

Claire erupted into laughter. Eliot looked at her confused.

"Wow, she's one for the books, Eliot."

"Claire, I'm sorry. I…"

"Listen, what you did before you did this," she said letting the bed sheet drop to the floor and pointing to herself, "is completely none of my business. But, is Mrs. wine and cheese going to pose any future problems?"

Eliot walked over to Claire and reached to cup her face between his hands, but she stepped back before he could touch her.

"You didn't answer me. Again, are there going to be any future problems with this woman, Eliot? Is whatever you were doing with this woman going to be a problem for you to stop?"

"No. Hell no. That was... that was a mistake. That ceased to be the minute I saw you again, Claire."

They stood looking at each other for a long moment.

"Don't fuck with me Eliot, OK? Don't fuck with me. We're both too old for this type of shit."

"I swear to you. You are all I've ever wanted my entire life."

He walked to her and she put her arms around his waist. They kissed. Loud banging and kicking erupted at the front door.

"Handle it, Eliot," Claire said, wrapping herself up in the bed sheet and heading upstairs.

Marilyn stood at the door red and furious. Her morning mascara dripped with the tears from her eyes and resembled something from a Pollack painting. Her eyes and cheeks were puffy and her lips swollen. Eliot thought she looked like a mud-skipper fish. He wanted to laugh, but Marilyn, with both hands, pushed him hard in the chest and he stumbled back into the house.

"Whoa, whoa, have you lost your fucking mind?" Eliot said.

"You're an asshole, you're an asshole and I hate you. What makes you think you can do this kind of shit to people?"

"You're married for Christ-sake. What the hell did you think we were doing?"

"You said you cared about me. You said I was good for you."

Claire had dressed and now stood, bright and obvious in her flame red dress, her arms folded across her chest, at the top of stairs leaning against the wall, watching and listening.

"Yes, so? What does all that mean in light of the situation, Marilyn? Were you gonna leave your family and what, run away with me, move in? You knew what we were doing, so what is your problem?"

"I'm not some trashy fly-by-night whore, Eliot. Who the hell do you think you are? I don't just fuck anybody, you asshole. I have a family. Do you understand that? I'm not that woman, Eliot. I have a child, I'm successful, I have a life, and I shared my body with you, you asshole. My body, Eliot. My body!"

Claire swatted at a moth and watched it flutter backwards into the hallway. She straightened the dress over her legs and resumed her position against the wall.

Eliot placed his hands on Marilyn's shoulders and stepped close to her.

"Exactly," he said, "and now there won't be any more problems. Things can go back to normal and the way they were, right? You've got your family, you're right. That's all that there is now. Isn't it better that way? No more sneaking, no more lies, no more..."

"You arrogant fuck," Marilyn said, then pulled out a letter opener she had hid in the waistband of her yoga pants. She shoved the sharp end of the opener into the side of Eliot's shoulder. He screamed and jumped back from her, spun around and fell on his back yelling and crying.

"Oh shit," Claire said and ran to the bottom of the stairs, stopped, and stared wide-eyed back and forth between Eliot and Marilyn. Marilyn pounced on Eliot and started to pound him with her fist in his face and chest.

"Call the cops, call the cops," he shouted as he tried to protect himself from her blows.

Claire ran into the kitchen, grabbed her phone from her purse and dialed 911.

Claire sat on a stool at the kitchen counter with her purse on her lap. She stared into the sunlight coming through the bay window in the living room. Dust particles floated in the ray of light. The light made a blurry rainbow on the carpet, and the shadows of the moths on the inside and the outside of the window mixed together inside the rainbow-like, tiny, dark, amorphous clumps. From the hall bathroom, where Claire and Eliot had managed to lock her in, two police escorted Marilyn out. She was in handcuffs and she was crying hard and deep, apologizing to the police through her gasping. On a gurney from the living room, Eliot watched her walk past him. She didn't look at him. He winced as one of the two paramedics finished bandaging his shoulder.

"You'll meet me at the hospital, right?" he said turning to address

Claire.

"Yeah," she said softly.

Outside several of the neighbors watched as the police put Marilyn into the back of their squad car and the paramedics put Eliot into the ambulance. A few tried to position themselves to see into the house, but Claire closed the door. From the window she saw the ambulance and police car take off north toward the hospital and jail. She turned to get her purse from the kitchen counter so she could follow the ambulance, but noticed the dead moth by the hearth. She stood above it and stared at it. Once in a while she touched it with the tip of her shoe to move it a bit. She grabbed a Kleenex off the side table next to the recliner, picked up the moth and carried it to the bathroom to flush it. When she turned on the light in the bathroom, a slew of the insects scattered. She batted a few that flew close to her face. Most of them escaped out into the hall, but a group of them stayed in the bathroom. She watched as they fluttered around the ceiling light. A few landed and crawled across the ceiling. She managed to grab one out of the air. She held it inside of her fist and felt its tiny legs moving against her palm. She grabbed the creature with her other hand and held it up to the light by its wings. The slick, downy fur of its wings came off on her fingers. She peered at its tiny, black eyes for a long moment. The dark, blank eyes stared back. She shuddered and released it. It darted away into the hall.

The click of her heels on the hardwood floor echoed loudly as she walked across the kitchen. She grabbed her purse and peeked out the blinds to make sure the crowd had dispersed then left the house. The neighbor to the right of Eliot's house was still out in his yard watering the lawn. He stared at Claire as she came out of the house. She smiled at him. He didn't respond but continued to watch her as she strutted across Eliot's driveway, got into her car and drove south out of the neighborhood.

The Bathers

The pool was situated in a small alcove in the lagoon, whose shore was surrounded by a rocky cliff barricaded behind a massive, stone wall. The wall was ancient and spanned the entire lagoon until it opened up into a vast, restless ocean. Although time and the salty winds and waters of the ocean had assailed the wall and battered holes and cracks where small crabs, sea worms, and mollusk now lived and scavenged upon each other, the wall still stood firm. It was green and brown and yellow from generations of algae and creatures that had lived, died, and been enmeshed in its sturdy surface by waves from the tumultuous ocean. No one knew when the wall had been built or who built it or why, and it was of no particular interest to the boy and girl who met at the pool everyday under its shadow to be together.

It was a deep, warm pool and the boy liked to dive off the carved onyx head of a salamander that protruded from the ebony wall that surrounded the pool. No one knew who the sculptor was or why the head had been carved from the black stone cliff that surrounded the pool. The salamander's mouth was open and a steady stream of water poured from it into the pool. The girl watched the boy balance himself on the shiny head of the sculpture. She stared at the thin muscles that had begun to develop recently and etched themselves through his smooth black skin. She rolled onto her side so that she could see him without the glare of the early morning sun that turned the water of the pool and the stream into silver. The boy flexed and stretched his body to make himself limber and resilient; the girl stretched hers for a reason she did not understand. She watched him arch and bound from the glistening head of the salamander, fall through the air like a shooting star, and slice the surface of the silver water with the precision of an arrow. She felt a warmth spread over her skin as if she had jumped into the water herself. It was a feeling she had begun to experience whenever she was around the boy, an urgent feeling that seemed to creep up from the beneath the ground and seep into her like a something molten and alive.

She had known the boy since they were young children and had played in the coconut groves under the watchful eyes of their mothers. She had always sought his company and enjoyed being around him; she had felt safe around him. He was older and bigger, and stronger than her, but she had at times felt that he was somehow weaker and not as smart as she was. She sometimes felt that she needed to take care of him. But lately she was feeling something different for him. He seemed to grow more mysterious and even a bit dangerous to her. It was nothing that he did, just the way that she had begun feeling. When she saw him she wanted to touch him. They had explored each other's bodies when they were younger but it was with the same interest that they had looked at the dead snakes and birds they found in the grove. But this feeling was stronger, intense and even selfish; she wanted to feel his skin and how it differed from hers, to have his body close to hers so that she could smell the earth in his hair and kiss the sun from his flesh. She wanted to feel his presence pressed against her, as well as the warmth that radiated from it. She wanted his flesh to cover hers to stop it from aching, yearning. She wanted to feel his body to break out of her own.

The boy's raven skin glistened when he emerged from the pool. Sand stuck to the bottom of his feet as he approached the girl stretched out on the white sands of the beach. The delicate curves of her arms, breasts, hips, and legs entranced the boy. He felt the familiar movement of his sex as he looked at the girl. He became bold with lust and awkward with nervousness and embarrassment. He ran to her and grabbed her in a mock tackle. She laughed and rolled over. He felt his sex brush against her thigh and moved off her quickly to hide it by pressing it into the sand. He had been close to her body for years and thought nothing of it. When they had been children and she kissed him once, he had pushed her away and made her cry. He had found the chasing and capturing of sand crabs and turtles more interesting than anything the girl could do. Now, every night he touched himself and imagined the girl naked and pressing her body against him, he imagined his fingers delving into her and her hand around him, squeezing and pulling. He wanted to cover her with his entire body. He felt the urge to protect her and possess her. He felt confused and frustrated because he didn't know why chasing frigatebirds with sticks wasn't as interesting as the girl anymore. Something about this made him feel weak and angry and he thought about never seeing the girl again, but the image of her body would soon crowd out the thought.

She called him silly and smacked him lightly on his back. He flicked a pebble at her, and reached to push her on the shoulder but missed and touched her breast. She looked at him and he stared at his hand. He began to gently knead her breast, and she closed her eyes and leaned her head back. A red-breasted musk parrot squawked in the distance. The boy positioned his body over the girl and began to remove her bikini as she reached up and pulled down his trunks. A wave washed upon them as they embraced. Outside the lagoon the ocean churned.

The boy discovered the statues in the middle of the lagoon. The two of them had begun to swim outside of the pool and find new places to make love. They coupled amongst the papaya, hibiscus, coconut and star fruit trees along the shores of the lagoon, in caves hidden behind fissures in the ancient wall and in the amethyst waves of the lagoon. He dove one day to catch a lobster for their lunch, and swam out further than he ever had. On the lagoon floor surrounded by a ring of red coral stood two statues of women carved from alabaster.

The boy had never seen anything like these women. Their pale skin glowed through the aqua-blue haze of the water. They were tall as the palm trees he climbed to get coconuts, and they were naked. The boy was transfixed. Their huge, white bodies were carved in exquisite detail. Their arms were outstretched as if opened to receive a lover. Their breasts were as big as his head and their sex was hairless. He had to touch them. He swam to the surface to catch his breath. When he broke the plane of the water he could see the girl on the beach. She waved to him. He did not wave back, but dove back straight away to see the alabaster women again.

He swam to the first woman and touched her hair. It was smooth and slick from algae, but the boy enjoyed the way his hands and arms slipped through the curving, spiraling twist of its flowing length. He swam to the other statue and brushed its lips with his fingertips. They too were smooth and slick, but he was amazed at their thinness. He swam the full length of the statue's face with his fingers gliding along its mouth. He swam back to the first statue and grabbed a huge breast with both hands. He ran his hands over the breast as if he were forming a bowl on his father's potting wheel. He held the tip of his sex against the tip of the giant nipple. Then he swam with the joy and speed of a porpoise toward the sex of the other statue. He pressed his entire body along its vertical length and swam slowly between the statues legs, his hands pressing and sliding across the thing's thighs and backside. He needed air. He swam back to the beach with one purpose in mind. When he reached the girl he pounced upon her. He made love to her with a force and fury neither of them had ever experienced. When they finished the girl laid on her back looking up into the cloudless blue sky. She liked the warmth of the sun upon her face. The boy lay with his head on her belly and thought about the alabaster women.

That night the boy could not think of anything else but the smooth white bodies of the statues. He snuck out of the village and ran through the jungle lit by the silver light of the moon. He raced across the beach to the lagoon, the craggy stone wall reached high beyond the light of the moon into the height of the night sky. The salamander stared out over the lagoon into the darkness beyond where the ocean churned.

The boy dove straight away into the water.

The thin light of small jellyfish, bobbing around the statues, lit their bodies with a hazy blue glow. The entire night the boy swam naked among the statues. Three times he spent himself on various places of the statues' bodies. As he swam back to shore, the boy felt happier than he ever had. The statues, their arms outstretched in welcome, would be there for him whenever he wanted them.

Every night, and often during the day the boy would visit the statues. He began to avoid the girl and made excuses as to why they could not spend the day together. He began to not want to make love to the girl. The girl's skin seemed dark and rough to him. Her mouth and lips fat and her backside wide and protruding. He would often shout at her and stomp off into the forest. This worried the girl. She did not know how or why she had angered the boy.

One night she followed the boy to the lagoon. From a dark outcropping of coral, she watched him, illuminated by the light of the jellyfish, do the things he did with the statues. The girl did not stay to watch the whole night. She felt as if her heart had disappeared from her body. When she reached the beach, she saw the salamander staring out over the lagoon into the darkness where the ocean churned. She cried as she plodded back to the village through the darkness of the jungle.

She did not seek the attention of the boy the next day or the day after that. She began to feel a different feeling. The feeling of her chest being empty was replaced with a feeling that fire burned inside of it. All she could think about was the pale white bodies of the alabaster statues, and when she thought about the pale naked bodies the fire grew in her chest. The girl began to shout at others in the village and hit her younger brothers and sisters. The others in the village did not know how or why they made the girl so angry.

One night the girl followed the boy to the lagoon again. After he had spent his time with the statues and left the lagoon, the girl dove into the water and swam to the statues. She had brought with her a hard black stone from the wall and all night she chipped away at the features of the statues. When she was done, the statues looked old, and craggy, and destroyed like the stones in the wall. The girl did not feel happy as she thought she would. She held her empty chest and walked slowly back to the village through the moonlit jungle.

On another day, some years after the boy and girl had first come to the lagoon beneath the wall, a different boy and girl walked amongst the papaya, hibiscus, coconut and star fruit trees along the shores of the lagoon. They chased each other in and out of the caves hidden behind fissures in the ancient wall and swam in the amethyst waves of the lagoon. One day the girl watched the boy balance himself on the shiny head of the salamander. She stared at the thin muscles that had begun to develop recently and etched themselves through his smooth black skin. She rolled onto her side so that she could see him without the glare of the early morning sun that turned the water of the pool and the stream into silver. The boy flexed and stretched his body to make himself limber and resilient; the girl stretched hers for a reason she did not understand. She watched him arch and bound from the glistening head of the salamander, fall through the air like a shooting star and slice the surface of the silver water with the precision of an arrow. After the boy disappeared into the water, the girl stared at the salamander that seemed to watch out over the water, past the lagoon out to where the ocean churned.

Residents in Eden

On April 7th, 2016:

Inside Maria Durant a million possibilities vie for the chance to be realized. Only one will accomplish this goal. She is unaware of this fierce struggle. She lies in her bed, eyes closed, in the arms of her lover. It is dark and her head lies on his chest. She listens to his slow steady breathing and it calms her, she moves closer to him. She is aware of every movement of his body; she feels his right leg underneath her leg and how it slightly spasms as his muscles begin to relax along with the rest of him. He is warm against her flesh and caresses her shoulder with slow, soft circular touches. Inside Maria Durant the struggle has turned into a microscopic reenactment of the situation that produced it. Inside Maria Durant two cells collide in an act that is both fusion and fracture; a hundred million others will disappear unrealized–slipping back into abstraction. The information carried in the sperm mixes with the information in the ovum and the process begins: ancient conversations take place in a chemical language; it is the original language in the strictest sense. Inside Maria Durant is the recreation of a pre-primordial event. Cellular division begins and the most repeated act in the history of existence happens again. Just like so many other things happen.

In Denver, Colorado, Marlon Driscoll pulled into a Conoco station to get gas and fill his right, front tire with air. It was payday; he had just gotten off work and was headed to the bar to get drunk. Marlon hated his job and loved his beer. His job was stifling, boring, and unfulfilling. He worked at a lumberyard, in the office doing data entry. The work wasn't hard; most of the time he sat around reading the newspaper, or scribbling down ideas he planned to turn into a book one day. He made enough money to pay his bills and keep him in beer and cigarettes. It was Friday and he wanted to escape into the ether of the night. He stared out onto to the street as he pumped his gas. He watched the people walking up and down the street in the fading light of dusk. The twilight didn't transform the street tonight. The homeless were just homeless, the drunks and junkies were just drunks and junkies, the lechers, lechers, whores, whores, gangstas', gangstas', and the hustlers, just hustlers. The cloud of night was devoid of magic, he thought. It had actually been devoid of magic for the last two years; the escape was only a habit now. He just didn't know what else to do anymore. He felt something in his head pop right at the temple. A feeling of dread and hopelessness enveloped him. The gas pump stopped but he still held onto the handle until he felt the gas pouring over his hand. He put the handle back on the pump, paid, filled his tire, got in his car and drove. He drove past the bar; he drove past his apartment, where his girlfriend sat on the couch in a methamphetamine delirium waiting for him to get home. He drove until the sun came up, well past the hour for him to be at work. He drove into New Mexico and didn't stop until he found himself in front of the motel El Corazón in Gallup, New Mexico.

In Springfield, Massachusetts, Evan Wong walked into his house. His wife and kids were gone. They were out of town visiting her mother. He had the house to himself. He tossed his coat on the couch and surveyed the living room. His wife had cleaned up before she left. He smiled and walked into the dining room. There was a note on the table next to a pack of cigarettes and a bottle of scotch. Have fun. I know you're going to do it anyway so I bought you these little gifts. Please just smoke on the back porch, it takes forever for the house to air out after you smoke. I made you dinner for a couple of nights; you're going to have to fend for yourself after Wednesday. I left mom's number on the fridge. I'll call you tonight when we get there. Love you. Talk to you soon. At the bottom of the letter, scribbled in green and red colored pencil, was a note from his kids that looked like it read we love you daddy. He carried the bottle into the kitchen, fixed a glass of ice and poured himself a double shot. Then he went upstairs and changed his clothes.

He sat outside and smoked his cigarette. The smoke tasted good and the warmth of it mixed with the warmth in his chest from the scotch. He sat with his feet propped up against the grill and watched the sun setting. A brilliant display of orange and blue streaked the sky. Evan was content. He did not miss his family at that moment. He loved them; he loved them dearly and would not change anything about his life. But, it had been a long time since he had spent any time alone, and he was thoroughly enjoying himself. He knew he would miss his wife's body next to him that night, but he would also get to stay up late and read without feeling guilty about keeping the light on. He would miss getting up in the morning and watching the kids rush around the house and the hugs and kisses, the yelling, the spilled cereal on the carpet, but he would be able to sleep late. He felt there was something intrinsically sublime about being alone. He felt complete with his family, and would feel incomplete without them; but he was complete alone as well, satisfied, happy. A cool breeze began to blow. Evan took a sip of his drink, pulled an old blanket over his legs and watched the sky turn into night.

In Glendale, Arizona, Karen Hodges woke up next to her husband Eddie. She lay on her back staring up at the ceiling, slowly, and reluctantly slipping out of sleep. She listened to Eddie's breathing. It was hard and raspy, as if he were gasping for his last breath. She closed her eyes tight and turned onto her side. Eddie snorted. She opened her eyes again and stared at her reflection in the mirrored glass of their closet door. She followed the contours and dips of her body underneath the white comforter. It reminded her of the striped mined hills she saw in Arkansas when she was a kid. She stared at her face. The skin under her eyes was darker than she remembered; the skin on her cheeks looser, not much, she thought, but enough that I notice. She tried to remember when she started to look different. She tried to remember when she had looked any different from the way she looked now. She thought she remembered a person she seemed to have known years ago. A woman, a younger woman. But she wasn't quite sure if that woman had ever really existed or if that woman was a woman she wished she had known or had been. Eddie rolled over with a grunt; his foot lodged in the small of her back. The muscles in her back tightened. She remembered a younger woman who had been inspired by ideas, who could sit for hours and watch the calm stillness of a lake, or who could be transformed by a painting or a poem. Eddie pushed his calloused heel into her butt. She slapped at his feet beneath the comforter. The calloused foot rubbed hard against the cellulite of her thighs. "Goddamn it Eddie move over," she said. He grunted and slid his foot down her leg. She turned over to move away from the foot and pulled the comforter off him. She looked at his body. She followed his curves. That's funny, she thought, that I should think of him as curved now. She followed his large, soft curves from his neck to his round, soft, curved shoulders. She poked his right shoulder and made a face as her finger sank into his flesh. She poked his shoulder twice, three times, four times, each time a little harder. She was a little amused by the way his skin sprang back like a piece of potato bread. Eddie grunted and rolled over. She watched his stomach roll with him. For a minute she was reminded of a National Geographic episode she had seen about walruses. She sat up, fluffed the pillows behind her back, and looked around the room. What she first saw were Eddie's pants, forty-four-inch waist, thirty-four length, draped over the back of the old reclining chair. Eddie's brother had given it to him on their wedding day. She had hated the chair then, but hated it even more now. The fiberglass stuffing was coming out at the seam in the left arm. The leather was worn through in spots and it was discolored and falling apart. She had wanted to throw the thing out ten years ago, but he wouldn't let her because it was still comfortable. He never even sits in the damn thing unless it's to pass out after he's been drinking, she thought. She looked over at the chest of drawers. Her make-up bottles and lipstick were open, dried out and scattered among his old credit-card receipts, toothpicks, snot rags, car keys, wallet, and miscellaneous pieces of paper. The drawers were half open with the straps of bras and the frayed elastic of jockey shorts hanging out. Eddie scratched his ass and scooted closer to her. Then something happened inside Karen Hodges. She looked down at Eddie as if he were a stranger. A vague fear swept over her and she felt as if she were alone, enclosed in a dark, black box with something black and seething, pulsating and sliding underneath her feet. Something old and unnamable, something outside the realm of human imagination. She slid back down under the comforter and rolled up into a fetal position clenching her eyes closed tight.

Five miles off the coast of Algiers, Algeria in the Mediterranean Sea, Al-Sa'id Hejaz sat lounging on the bow of his boat. His nets were cast and he looked out over the water. It was a balmy day and the clouds moved slowly across the sky like a herd of grazing animals. The water was calm and the boat drifted lazily. Al-Sa'id closed his eyes and began to drift off to sleep. He was woken up by a splash near the boat. He turned over and looked over the bow. He could see the circle of waves where something had jumped out of the water. He was hoping it was mackerel and his haul would be good today. He turned back over to go to sleep when he heard another splash. He stood up and saw a large black fish about three and a half feet long shoot up out of the water about two feet.

When that one landed another one jumped, this one close enough that Al-Sa'id could feel the spray of water. Two, three, four more fish darted out of the water. Soon they were jumping all around the boat and Al-Sa'id began to get nervous. A fish landed on the bow right at Al-Sa'id's feet. It was shaped like a baseball bat, all black and about three feet long with a long, sail-like dorsal fin. It had large silver eyes and a mouth full of small pointy teeth. Al-Sa'id had never seen a fish that looked like that before and he had fished these waters for forty years. The fish began to flop around, it made Al-Sa'id nervous and he kicked it overboard. More fish began to jump and another two or three landed in the boat. Al-Sa'id looked at the sea and it had turned black with the fish. There were so many of them they were squirming over each other out of the water. Al-Sa'id began to get frightened. He backed away from the bow, close to the cabin. The boat began to move with violent jerks, hard enough to make Al-Sa'id stumble across the deck. He saw his nets being stretched out. The boat began bobbing up and down, the bow left the surface of the water. Al-Sa'id crawled across the deck to unhook the net before the boat was capsized. As he reached the railing, he watched several of the fish fly out of the water as if they were thrown. Then a giant fin like that of a whale broke the surface of the water, and for a minute Al-Sa'id thought he saw a huge set of teeth skim the surface. He jumped up and stumbled backwards onto the deck. Scooting backwards like a crab, he rested against the wall of the cabin. His eyes were wide and sweat covered his forehead; he could feel his heart pounding in his chest. In front of him he saw something rise up out of the water. The black fish jumped around it like water on a hot skillet. Slowly a monstrous, black back, rising at least twelve feet out of the water, with bony ridges and smooth skin, glided in front of the boat then slowly descended back into the water. Al-Sa'id sat silent and stared out over the sea. He did not move, only his eyes darted back and forth. He did not move even after the swarm of fish dissipated and the sea returned to the calm smoothness it had been before. He only watched his net, tattered and floating out to sea.

In Casper, Wyoming at the Penrose Retirement Center, Eleanor Harmon watched Winston Munce walking up the path from the garden. He was wearing the same brown trousers he wore all the time, pulled up past his navel. He shuffled up the path slow but steady, his socks showing beneath the leg of his pants. The tail of his red, plaid shirt hung out of his pants in the front. Eleanor smiled. Winston looked up and saw her; he waved and she stood up and waved back. Eleanor was seventy-seven, but she looked ten years younger. She had been a dancer all her life and had been married to a photographer. She had moved back to Wyoming, where she was originally from, after her husband died. She was well-off and had planned to take up painting, until she got in a car accident. An injured hip put her, by her own decision, in Penrose. She had been there for two years when she met Winston. "You look wonderful," Winston said, taking her hand and holding it gently between his hands. "Thank you, Winston," she said, placing her free hand over his hands. They looked into each other's eyes for a moment, smiling. "Here, here sit down, take a seat, it's hot out today," she said, guiding him into the chair next to hers. There was a pitcher of water on a table next to her and she poured them both a glass. They sat in silence for a while looking out over the courtyard. "There's a new one," she said, pointing to the hummingbird feeder. "Mm hmm," Winston said, nodding his head. He was looking down at his pants, scratching at a cigarette burn on the pocket. "I made this for you," he said reaching into his pocket and taking out a small book. He handed it to Eleanor. It was a chapbook. *Poems for Eleanor* was the title. She looked up from the book at him with a look of surprise, questioning. "I finished them about two months ago. I been writin' 'em for about a year now. You know, for you." She stared at him. "I don't know what to say. Thank you so much. I didn't know you wrote poetry, Winston." "Not for about twenty years now. Well, until now of course. I went an' got that printed up at Egan's. Well what'd ya think, you gonna read one?" Eleanor opened the book to the middle and read. When she finished she looked at him, he could see that her eyes were wet. "You like it?" "Winston, it's..." "I love you Eleanor." Tears slid gently down her face, past the corner of her smile. "I love you too, Winston, I do." She leaned towards him and he brought his forehead down so she could kiss it. "I started again 'cause of you. I ain't wrote anything in years. Didn't feel much. Eleanor, I ain't been too much in my life. Married twice, drank too much at times, divorced twice. I didn't have much of a job, the last one anyway, the one I kept the longest. I wasn't much, Eleanor, you know what I mean. I don't have much of a relationship with my boy. I don't have much money, Eleanor. But, I'm here and we're both here and you mean so much to me and I know I'm older than you, and I'm not so handsome..."

"Yes, Winston. Yes I will."

He stopped talking and looked away at the bird feeder. He was silent for a moment, but she could see that his eyes were wet. He turned back to her and stared into her eyes. He smiled. She smiled. "I love you Winston Munce."

In The Olympic Mountains National Park in Washington, Carlin Leebon sat on the bank of a small stream watching it empty into a small pond. He had found this niche about forty yards off the trail. He heard the soft gurgling of the stream and followed the sound to the space. It was like an outdoor sanctuary, a primeval landscape untouched by time. It was a clearing covered in shadow by a ring of evergreens that he could not even see the top of. The ground was wet and black and covered with light green moss. The dirt yielded to his foot when he stepped on it. In the middle was the pond, surrounded by ferns, being fed by the thin stream in a steady, smooth, flow. He stood at the bank listening. The silence of the forest was intensified here. He felt a profound calmness. He took off his backpack and leaned it against an outcropping; he leaned down to the pond, a small silver fish darted away from him into the shadows of the other side of the bank; Carlin scooped the water up into his hands and drank. The water was clear and cold and he felt the coolness wash down his throat and through his body.

He sat with his back against a mound of dirt at the base of a huge evergreen, and fell asleep a few minutes later. He only slept for about fifteen minutes, but when he woke up he felt like he had slept a full eight hours. He was refreshed and alert, but he stayed at the pond instead of going back to the path. He decided it would be a great place to camp for the night. As he unpacked his gear he remembered the dream he had had while he was napping. He dreamt that he was walking down a path of golden sand with the Buddha. As they walked the Buddha talked to him about the Four Noble Truths, The Eight-Fold Path and The Secret of the Flower. He had never heard of these things but in his dream he understood them. Then they came upon an Indian woman sitting on a rock off to the side of the path. She was the most beautiful woman he had ever seen, and they stopped in front of her. The Buddha then began to tell him about the woman. He told him about every aspect of her life, about her joy, her pain, her sorrow, her dreams, her goodness, her wickedness, everything. Then Carlin asked the woman if all the things the Buddha had said were true. She said yes. She bowed her head to the Buddha and he bowed back, then Carlin and the Buddha continued on the path. Carlin asked the Buddha how he knew all those things about the woman. The Buddha said to know those types of things you have to be enormous. Then they walked in silence. They were coming to the shores of a vast lake; the sun was setting and the light reflected off the water in brilliant oranges and yellows. Then he woke up.

That night Carlin lit a very small fire and sat against the tree looking at the light flicker in the stream and pond. He watched the slow, steady, smooth flow of the stream empty into the pond. The flow was continuous, and even when he drifted off to sleep he could hear its soothing sound.

In Paradise, California, Noel Redding sat alone in his apartment. He was seventy-two years old. He sat in his reclining chair in his underwear. His undershirt was stained gray with dried beer and old pizza sauce; his shorts were stained brown in the front from old, dried piss. His skin was yellowish, the color of Dijon mustard, and he smelled bad. He was fully reclined in his chair and his belly seemed to rise up from the chair like an island. He scratched himself constantly, under the folds of the skin of his neck, the back of his head, his arms and legs, groin, everywhere. On a table next to the chair, situated so he didn't even have to extend his arm, was a table with a gallon bottle of vodka, it was more than three-quarters empty, a pack of cigarettes, a cracked, blue plate with some old unidentifiable moldy food, the TV remote, and a mixing bowl half full of spit and blood. He seemed to be asleep, but his head flopped from side to side. Sometimes he would lift his head and open his eyes and stare at the TV. His eyes were dark and glazed over and he groaned as he lifted his head, then would let it fall to one side or the other. The room was dark except for the hazy blue glow of the TV. Noel yelled out. It was a deep, thick bellow that made his jowls shake. A woman in the apartment next to his slammed her fist against the wall. "Shut-up ya old bastard, die why don't ya." A painting of a farmhouse fell off the wall and smashed on the floor.

Noel, in a fit struggled to get out of the chair, he growled and shook the chair in an effort to get out but was wracked with a bolt of pain across his torso; he fell back limp into the chair and yelled out again. "Shut up, for Christ fucking sake, shut up," the woman yelled. Noel sat grimacing, sweating, and biting his lower lip. Tears ran down his cheek and he whimpered under his breath. He closed his eyes. He wondered where his son was. He hadn't seen him in seventeen years. He wondered if his wife was still alive and where she was. He wondered what the weather was outside, what day it was, what time it was. A moan exploded from his mouth as if he were spitting something out. Angry with himself for letting his mind wander he yelled out again. Four loud slams against the wall. Noel yelled louder, threw the TV remote at the wall, then fell into a fit of coughing. He grabbed the mixing bowl and spit out three globs of thick, ropy blood. He grabbed the vodka, drank, swished it around his mouth and swallowed. He fell back into the chair with a groan, holding his stomach and biting his lip. He reclined into the chair and closed his eyes. Four hours later, like so many other things that happen, Noel Redding died.

In Natchez, Mississippi, Zachary Jackson's mother took him to see Reverend Eli Washington. Reverend Eli was an evangelist and a healer. Zach was ten years old; he was handicapped—paralyzed on the entire right side of his body because of a stroke he had had during his delivery. He could not speak because his vocal chords were damaged, his right eye was blind and clouded over with white, he had no right ear except for a deformed stub surrounding a small hole, and he could not walk.

The reverend walked slowly onto the stage. He was supported on either side, his wife on his left and his son on his right. They were all dressed in white; the reverend wore a three-piece tuxedo, his son wore one too, and his wife a flowing, lacy evening gown. He stepped up to the pulpit and his family sat down on either side of him in chairs. The crowd moved forward. Seven big men in suits and sunglasses spread out in front of the stage, arms crossed, staring at the crowd. The reverend began to speak. He spoke about the goodness of God, he spoke about the power of God, he spoke about the sins of man and the suffering for the sins of man, he talked about the forgiveness of God, he spoke about the weakness of man and how he must return unto the Lord for salvation. He spoke about how he had sinned and about how he had been saved and then chosen by God to work God's miracles. He told the people that they must believe in the power of God and the power that worked through him. Then he told the people that if they truly believed in the power of God, and they truly believed that he was God's messenger and servant then, to come unto him and let the power of God heal them. Then the reverend's son and wife came to his sides and helped him down the stairs of the stage. The crowd moved forward in a wave. Shouts and screams of praise and remorse floated above the crowd. Tears ran down their faces and people called out to God and the reverend to save them. The big men in the suits made people form a line. One of the men handed the son a microphone and the son held it for the reverend to speak into. The reverend began to speak in tongues. Mrs. Jackson dropped to her knees in front of Zach's wheelchair holding her son's hands and rocking back and forth crying and praising God's name. Her sister stood behind her and gently rubbed her shoulders, she pointed to the reverend, Mrs. Jackson looked up, the reverend was waving them forward. She wheeled Zach in front of the reverend and he placed his hands upon the boy's head, bowed his own head and began speaking in tongues again. He began talking faster and faster and his body began to shake, Zach began to shake too. Mrs. Jackson watched her son, her eyes wide and staring and her mouth agape. An ear popped out of the deformed nub on the side of Zach's head like a flower blossoming in the morning. The milky white film over his eye disappeared, and the boy stood up and walked over to his mother and said, "I love you, momma." Then the reverend stopped, one of the men escorted Zach and his family off to one side in view of the crowd. The crowd cheered and cried and screamed the name of God. They began to push forward, and the men in the suits had to hold some of them back. Mrs. Jackson hugged her son and fell to her knees again; she clasped her hands together and held them up to the sky, "Thank you Lord, oh Lord Jesus, thank you God." She ran over to the reverend and hugged him tightly. He held her hands in his and smiled at her. The man in the suit gently pulled her away.

Fifteen miles southeast of Kuala Terengganu in Malaysia, at the America's Super Sports Shoe factory an eleven-year-old girl works in the factory. No one has asked or knows her name except her eighty-six-year-old grandmother and her eight other siblings. She is a thin girl; you can see her ribs beneath her skin. Her teeth are rotting out of her mouth, and her full lips are cracked and dry. Her big, dark eyes stare out of her face like dull, glass orbs. The child works in the shoe factory thirteen to sixteen hours a day to support her family. She makes the equivalent of about two dollars and seventeen cents a week in American currency. She sews the tongue into tennis shoes all day. Sometimes, more often than not, when the demand is heavy she and her fellow workers are forced to work even longer hours. They are locked in the factory until the job is complete.

Her supervisor walks up behind her while she works. She does not turn around or move away from her work. He just stands behind her silently watching her; then he taps her on the shoulder. She gets up from her table and follows him into a room. He closes the door and the child begins to undress. She doesn't cry or fight anymore; she knows he'll beat her and then she'll miss work. She just hopes he doesn't call the other men in today and that he is quick. When he's on top of her she thinks about her grandmother.

Her grandmother tells her about when her mother and father were young and they farmed the land. She tells her about when the army came and took the land and killed her mother and father and grandfather because they did not want their land taken and they protested against the army. She told the child about how it was good once the factory came because the army left and quit killing people. So the girl works every day at the shoe factory, so the army won't come back again.

When he finishes he throws her a dirty rag and tells her to clean up and get back to work. She does as she's told.

In Wyoming, Delaware, Reverend Elsa Witiless pauses in silence and stares out over her congregation. They are all staring back at her, silent and wide-eyed, some with their mouths agape. She knows she's got them right where she wants them. Now it's time to save their souls, she thinks. "The Devil," she yells out slamming her fist on the pulpit, startling several children in the front rows and causing a baby to cry. "Satan is the bringer of death, Satan is the taker of life, it's the devil that took Mr. Hadley here. God wants us to live so that we can worship him and love him. It's the devil that wants to take us from life, from God. It's the devil that tries to steal our souls after he takes our life. Death is not natural! God is the giver of life not the taker. Satan killed Mr. Hadley. And may God rest his soul and protect it from Satan. I'm angry now, I'm angry at death. Why did Mr. Hadley, here, lying in this coffin, why did Mr. Hadley have to die? He was a good man, I knew him, and you knew him. Why would God take him like he did? No! No! It wasn't God it was the devil. And now he's got me mad and I hope he's got you mad, 'cause he's out there bettin' on your souls too, right now, hear me now, I speak the truth. I need you to get mad with me, I need you to raise your fist in anger against death, against Satan himself." She stood in front of the pulpit with her arms raised. Several older people were standing up in their pews with their arms raised too. Another baby began to wail and small children scooted close to their mothers and fathers and held them. A little boy in the second row with tears streaking down his face howled and clawed at his grandmother as she stood up with raised hands. Reverend Elsa yelled out. "I renounce you Satan, I renounce your death!" The congregation repeated her words. She swayed back and forth on the altar. "Pray with me children, pray for Mr. Hadley's soul, pray for your children's souls, and pray for your own souls! Pray to God for forgiveness that you may be saved from eternal death!" The little boy in the second row clung to his grandmother's leg, he was trembling and her skirt, crumpled up to her thigh, stuck to the child's face from his tears. He moaned and shoved his face into her hip.

Reverend Elsa went back behind her pulpit and fell silent again. She bowed her head and whispered into the microphone. "Please join me now in a silent prayer for the salvation of Mr. Hadley's soul."

In Brazil, about fifty miles south of Xingu and about fifty miles north of Rio Branco, is a tributary from the Purus River. And along that tributary is a lagoon where an undiscovered species of millipede lives. It has lived there in its present from for over three hundred thousand years, unseen by human eyes. Six hundred miles northeast along the Amazon River is a rubber processing plant. Chemicals from the plant, as yet undiscovered, have seeped into the river and are starting to affect the ecosystem. Before the chemical is discovered it will decimate a species of bird, the nightjar, because the chemical will adversely affect the reproductive system in the female black currant grasshoppers, which is the main food source for the nightjars. The chemical will also cause cancer in a species of fern, cause over-population of the dwarf pencil fish, because their main predator, the fresh water dolphin will decrease in numbers. The toxin will also affect the reproductive organs of the millipede. But something will happen. Like so many other things happen. A gene will mutate in a female that is hatched. It is a gene that will produce an enzyme that will attack the lethal toxin and convert it into nourishment. An architect in Oaxaca, Mexico will discover the millipede ten years later in a box of cornflakes.

The Anthropologist

On the girl's 2nd birthday her father disappeared. He got up from the dinner table where his wife and his mother had their usual power struggle, each looking at him in turns for a sign of recognition or support. He didn't acknowledge either and stared at his father, who, with his mouth slightly open and a glazed-over look in his eyes, stared into the television. He looked around the room, then stared at his hands, then stared around the room, then rubbed his hands on his pants until the skin of the calluses on his palms rubbed off into tiny balls. His wife and mother stared at him. He brushed the skin off his pants, chuckled, nodded at the two women, and got up from the table. They watched him leave, then started their diatribe again.

The girl's father went into her room and stared at her as she slept. He caressed her downy hair and smiled as tears welled in his eyes. He picked her up and she opened her groggy eyes and smiled. He held her to his chest and she nestled her head in the crook of his neck. He took two silver balls from his shirt pocket. One was the size of a sunflower seed; the other was the size of a peanut. He put the peanut sized ball in his mouth and swallowed it, then he pushed the other one into the girl's mouth and made her swallow. The old hoodoo man in the French Quarter had told him they would work. He believed him. "So I can feel everything you feel and you can feel everything I feel, always," he said, then hugged her, kissed her, and set her back in the crib. No one ever saw him again after that day.

The girl grew up with a cheery and bright disposition. She was an intelligent child who was curious about everything. She involved herself in all kinds of activities; she played sports, was a cheerleader, a member of the chess club, a thespian; she learned to play the piano exquisitely. But there was a sadness that permeated everything. It wasn't an overwhelming intrusion, nor did it affect her to the point of disability; it was more like an ever-present melancholy, a longing for something she could not determine and that she could never break out of. It was something she kept to herself. She never cried or indulged in the feeling, but sometimes in her room she felt a wetness on the side of her face and tasted tears that were not her own. Afterwards in the center of her stomach a tiny pinpoint of warmth would seem to radiate inside her. It made her feel comfortable for a moment, long enough to forget about the sadness.

She went to a prestigious college and graduated in Anthropology with honors. She traveled all over the world digging up secrets of the past. She eventually got married and had children of her own, but the sadness still lingered. She became a grandmother, and it still lingered.

The woman and her husband retired in Oregon. Out of all the places in the world that she had been to, Oregon had appealed to her the most. She loved her house on the lake, her garden with the snap dragons, sunflowers, and gardenias; she loved the way the sun set silvery and warm behind the pine-laden hills. Oregon felt like home.

One day as she hiked in the forest behind her house, she came upon an old tattered shack overgrown with vegetation. Being an anthropologist, she was of course intrigued. The shack was an anteroom for a lodging that went back deep into a cave. Pictures were painted on the walls of the cave in oil paints. The pictures were of places she had been, things that she had done. There was a picture of her first piano recital, a picture of both her graduations, of a dig site in Kenya, Sri Lanka, and Bogota, of her marriage, the birth of her first child, and an unfinished one of her gardening. In a small alcove she discovered a skeleton in tattered clothes. It sat in a folding chair bent over a decomposing wooden table; the tendrils of creeper vines entwined through it's eye sockets and ribs. She examined the skeleton. It was a male who had not been dead more than about ten or fifteen years. On the seat was a small silver ball about the size of a peanut. She picked it up and examined it. She held it in the palm of her hand as if weighing it then she rolled it in a circle around her palm. She stared at it for a long moment, entranced. She sniffed it then put it in her mouth and swallowed it.

The next morning, she woke up with a warmth spreading from the center of her belly to every point of her body. She got up and looked at her husband, he looked more handsome than the first day she had met him. She opened the curtains and the day was bright. She felt light as if her body were made of air. She made coffee and sat on the porch and sipped it, smiling as she watched a flock of starlings dance across the sky.

Acknowledgements

Some of the pieces in this collection have previously appeared in the following publications:
"Pieces," and "Rain, Not Tears upon My Face," as "The Way the Rain Falls" in *Rio Grande Review*; "Residents in Eden" in *Wazee Journal* and *Metrosphere*; "And to Think I Saw It on Broadway" as "And to Believe I Saw It on Broadway" in *The Pedestal Magazine*.

I would like to thank all my friends and family who supported and encouraged me.

Many thanks to all the following, for their encouragement and help: Nick Arvin; Joseph Avski; the Faculty of the Creative Writing Department at The University of Texas at El Paso, especially Daniel Chacón; Carrie Chapman; Andrea Dupree, and the Lighthouse Writer's Workshop; Dr. Tyrone Jaeger; Sherry Jones; Shane D. Peterson, Renee Ruderman; and Ken Zeigler.

Special thanks to Laura Cesarco Eglin and Minerva Laveaga Luna at Veliz Books. (Thanks for putting up with all my annoying questions, Lau).

Infinite thanks to my mother, father, and sisters, and also to my Aunt Natalie "Bunny" Pichon, who was my first audience all those years ago.

All my love to Kaidyn.

About the Author

Trent D. Hudley is a professor of English. He teaches in the Creative Writing MA Program at Regis University; he also teaches at Metropolitan State University and the Community College of Denver. He earned his BA from Metropolitan State University and his MFA from the University of Texas at El Paso. He was raised in Denver, Colorado and before he entered the world of academia he held a multitude of positions including working in the *Denver Post* Sports Room, janitor, kitchen manager, painter, cashier, and a multitude of other similar jobs. He still lives in Denver in the company of his friends, family, and his daughter.